I0600778

THE FIRST TEN DAYS
second edition

Marleen Kunze

2D Fruit
Publishing

The First Ten Days, second edition

Copyright © 2008, 2018 Marleen Kunze

All rights reserved.

All Scripture quotations, unless otherwise indicated, are taken from the Holy Bible, New International Version®, NIV®. Copyright ©1973, 1978, 1984, 2011 by Biblica, Inc.™ Used by permission of Zondervan. All rights reserved worldwide. www.zondervan.com The "NIV" and "New International Version" are trademarks registered in the United States Patent and Trademark Office by Biblica, Inc.™

This novel is a work of fiction. Names, descriptions, entities and incidents included in the story are products of the author's imagination. Any resemblance to actual persons, events and entities is entirely coincidental.

Published by 2D Fruit Publishing
PO Box 8072
West Chester, Ohio 45069 USA
2dFruit.com

Book design copyright © 2018 2D Fruit Publishing. All Rights Reserved.
Cover design of first 2008 edition by Jeff Kunze
Cover adaptation and interior design for second edition by Mike Kunze

Published in the United States of America

ISBN: 978-0-9986950-4-4
1. Fiction: Religious
2. Apocalyptical category

Also by Marleen Kunze

Go back to a time in history when the Roman Empire controlled most of the world. One hundred thousand men spent their days at the Coliseum and other arenas watching vicious animal performances.

In Marleen Kunze's <u>Escape From Rome</u>, the adventure begins when the Coliseum manager's teenage sons witness a bloody performance and rescue a man about to be trampled and gored by rhinos. The fateful rescue angers the emperor and endangers the lives of Nolan's entire family.

Fleeing from the ruthless Emperor Domition, a handful of teenagers join the hunting team Nolan sends to Africa. As they trek around the Great Sea, they search for wild animals, and find survival and the truth about God.

Will the family escape from Rome and find the Christian faith they realize they are seeking? Or will they be captured by the the emperor's men and sent into the arena?

For purchasing options visit
https://MarleenKunze.com/EscapeFromRome

CHAPTER ONE

Tuesday, Day One

Matt Moses stared at the TV in disbelief. According to the TV station, people disappeared all over the world. A local reporter was describing an unusual scene, when a hysterical young man ran out onto the street. He was yelling, grabbed the microphone, and shouted, "Someone out there help me. My wife and three little children vanished right in front of my eyes. I searched the entire house. They are gone! Where did they go? Does anyone know?"

"Look around," replied the reporter. "Drivers disappeared right out of their cars. The paramedics are still working to get an eighty-year-old woman out of that SUV over there. She told the police that her husband disappeared and her car just plowed into that parked truck."

The show returned to the newsroom where the news team reported that people disappeared worldwide at 2:17 pm Eastern Time. They showed pictures from an overpass of the freeway where many vehicles without drivers left a trail of destruction. They featured a scene in Toronto where buildings were destroyed by a jet that lost its pilots and another in California, where a semi veered off the road and went into an elementary school building, killings hundreds of children who were sitting on the floor of the gymnasium for a school assembly. A frantic teacher reported that she noticed that some of the children disappeared just seconds before the huge truck burst through the wall.

Matt turned off the TV, confused and wondering if he was dreaming. This can't be happening. He opened the window and looked out. It was a beautiful, sunny, fall day. The breeze was blowing and the birds were singing. The squirrels were hopping around the yard, picking up acorns. Out in the country everything seemed fine. Maybe the TV network was playing a joke on the public to improve their ratings. He decided to call his daughter Sydney, who was out shopping with his wife Rosemary. Maybe they saw something. As he picked up his phone, he had a bad feeling, thinking that maybe one of those cars, missing the driver, ran into his wife and daughter.

The phone rang and rang. It went to the message. Matt hung up and called again. It rang a few times and the phone clicked on. "Sydney. Are you there? Sydney. Answer me!" shouted Matt. He listened quietly then, thinking he could hear something.

"Matt. I'm hurt!" Rosemary said, barely whispering.

"Rosemary, what's wrong? Let me talk to Sydney if you are hurt." said Matt.

"She's gone. Sydney's gone. She left me alone in the car and it hit a tree," Rosemary said. "Help me Matt."

"Rosemary, are you still there? Where are you?" Matt yelled. Matt realized that Sydney was probably among those who disappeared. Why would Sydney disappear? She wasn't into anything weird. Why her?

When Rosemary didn't talk anymore, Matt turned the TV back on, and saw some local scenes before him, the huge pileup on the highway and a fiery path left by a jet that slid through town. Suddenly Larry, Sydney's husband burst through the front door. "I had a heck of a time getting here," he said. "Most of the roads are clogged. People must be driving crazy out there. Where's Sydney?"

Matt stared at Larry with tears in his eyes. "She's missing. People all over the world are missing. It looks like Sydney is one of them.

"What in the world is going on? Why would people disappear?" asked Larry.

"I don't know," said Matt. "It's like a bad dream. But Rosemary is alone somewhere out there in the car. She's hurt and unconscious. I have her on the cell phone, but she's not talking now. Do you know your license number, Larry?

Larry stood there a moment, like he was in shock. Then the tears poured out of him and he started sobbing. Matt put his arms around him and they cried together.

"She's been my girl since the fifth grade," said Larry. "And you were like my father since then."

"Well that part is not going to change," said Matt. "You are like one of my own kids, and Josh and Lori feel the same way, like you are their brother."

Suddenly Matt heard a sound on the line, then he heard sirens. Larry leaned in and listened too. "That sounds like a saw or drill," said Larry.

Finally a man's voice came on the phone. "Is anyone there?" asked the man.

"Yes, I'm Matt Moses. You must have found my wife Rosemary," Matt said. "Is she OK?"

The man answered hesitantly. "She's alive, but she's lost a lot of blood. I'm going to try to get her into one of these ambulances. Stay on the line and I'll let you know."

After what seemed like hours, the man came back on the phone. "Sir, the men are coming this way with a gurney. There are two purses here. Am I right that the driver disappeared?"

Matt and Larry looked at each other. Matt could hardly recognize his own voice as he realized that Sydney was really gone. "My daughter Sydney was driving. My wife said that she was gone."

"I'll send both purses to the hospital with your wife. I'm going to hang up now and put the phone in a purse," he said.

"Wait," Matt said. "Where is the car?"

"Trust me," said the man. "Your car is not drivable. If your daughter had not disappeared, she would be dead. I can see that the seatbelt is still fastened. Your wife will be at St. Ann's Hospital. Bye now."

"I didn't even get a chance to thank the man," said Matt as he put the phone down. "Now how are we going to get to the hospital? My car is dead and now your car is wrecked."

"Oh that's right," said Larry. "Sydney and I were going to take you and Rosemary car shopping tonight."

"Maybe Mom and Dad can loan us their car," said Matt. "Oh no. I should check on them!"

Just then Matt's son Josh charged in the door. "Dad, Grandma and Grandpa are gone! I was taking a nap on their brown sofa and then I was going to clean out their gutters. When I woke up, they were gone. Well I know Grandpa can't exactly get out of that hospital bed, so I thought that was pretty weird. I tried calling you, but the lines were busy for a long time. For some reason I turned on the TV and found out that people are missing all over the world. I am so glad you're still here Dad. You too Larry. Where's Mom?"

"She's on the way to St. Ann's Hospital. But Sydney is gone. I guess the car went out of control when she disappeared," said Matt.

Josh looked at Larry and realized that's why he looked so bad. "Oh no, not Sydney. What about Lori?"

"I'm sure Lori and Ken are fine. You know they sleep until 2:00 pm every day," said Matt. "I guess I can call them now without getting yelled at."

Matt dialed the number and it rang seven, eight, nine times. He thought they could be missing, but then Lori answered. "Hello."

"Lori. Are you guys all right?" Matt asked.

"Well, Dad, you woke me up ten minutes before my alarm went off. You know we have to go to work pretty soon," said Lori. Ken and Lori worked the afternoon shift at a 24-hour Walmart where they met. They worked every week day from four pm to midnight, and then they hung out at a bar until morning. After that they went home and slept until it was time to go to work the next day. They had no idea anything had happened. Matt quickly explained that Sydney and Grandma and Grandpa all disappeared, along with many people all over the world.

"Uh Dad, that's a lot to think about. I'll try to explain everything to Ken and we'll turn the TV on," said Lori.

"Wait a minute," said Matt. "I didn't tell you that your mom is at St. Ann's Hospital. Larry and I and maybe Josh are going to see her pretty soon."

"I'll call you back Dad," said Lori. "I have to tell Ken about all this." And she hung up.

"She didn't even ask how Mom is!" said Josh.

"You know, Josh," said Matt. "You haven't mentioned Allison. Did you call her to see if she's still around? Maybe she disappeared."

"She's not my problem anymore, and I don't care if she's dead or alive or disappeared. Seriously, I don't care," shouted Josh. Josh and Allison had lived together for two years. She had a problem with alcohol and practically lived at the local bars. Occasionally she didn't come home at night. Finally Josh had enough of that. He moved out of their place and into a little trailer near his job. Matt knew enough to drop the subject.

The phone rang and it was Lori. "Dad, we aren't going to work because the store will be closed all day. When the cashiers disappeared, the place was robbed. The managers locked up, but it won't open until they have tighter security. We're heading over to check on Ken's mom, and then we'll meet you at the hospital.

"That sounds good, Honey. Be careful. I hear the roads are very dangerous out there, and I don't want to lose any more of my children," Matt said.

"I'll be careful. Bye, Dad," said Lori.

Josh had been pacing around the room the entire time that Matt was on the phone with Lori. Finally he said, "Dad, remember I came here on foot from Grandma and Grandpa's. Do you want to wait while I go get my truck, and drive back here to go to the hospital? It will take a while."

"Oh, what do you think Larry?" asked Matt. "Should we just take a bus to the hospital?"

"Whatever you say," said Larry. "All I can think about is how I'm going to live without Sydney."

"OK, Josh, go get your truck," said Matt. "We can take the bus to the hospital, but it would be nice if you meet us there and bring us back home."

Matt knew he needed to keep Larry busy, but he had one more thing he needed to do. "You know I have to call my sister and tell her about Mom and Dad."

Matt called Melinda's number, but he got the answering service. "Hello. You have reached Jack and Melinda. We aren't home right now. Leave a message!" Matt noticed that he also had the numbers of their four married children, so he called them too. Nobody answered and he left messages for them too.

"Come on Larry. Let's go see how Rosemary is getting along," said Matt. He and Larry put on their jackets, locked the door, and walked to the bus stop.

"Matt do you think there is any chance we can get Sydney back?" asked Larry, crying again.

"I don't think so Larry, but this never happened before. I suppose it's possible," said Matt. So many things to think about. *Why did they disappear? Where are they?*

CHAPTER TWO

Matt and Larry rode the bus to the hospital. Many people on the bus were crying. In the hospital they found Rosemary in the emergency room. A doctor was there, checking her stitches. He realized that Matt was her husband, so he caught him up on her treatment.

"Hello Mr. Moses. Your wife has been a good patient. We gave her some blood and stitched up her head, arm, and leg. She doesn't have a concussion or any broken bones, so you can take her home. As you can see, there are many people we haven't even checked yet. We are short-handed because of all the employees who disappeared. I'm releasing her into your care. Make sure she gets plenty of rest and drinks lots of water," said the doctor. "And make sure you keep her warm. She's had quite a shock."

"Thank you doctor. We will take good care of her," said Matt. The doctor nodded at a woman who came over with a wheel chair. She helped Rosemary into the chair and had her sign the appropriate forms.

Matt spotted Lori and Ken in the doorway and Josh was coming up right behind them. Lori and Ken offered to take the whole group in their minivan, and soon they were back on the roads, driving around wrecked cars, water shooting out of fire hydrants, and broken poles and road signs.

"I'm hungry," said Josh. "Lots of places are closed, but I did see a McDonalds open just up the street. We're heading right for it."

They searched Sydney's purse and found enough money to feed the whole family. They went through the drive-thru and took their food to Matt and Rosemary's house. Everyone went in and sat around the TV eating. The disappearances took place everywhere in the world and so did the resulting chaos. Planes, trains, boats, cars, and motorcycles lost their drivers. Crashes were everywhere.

Finally Josh spoke up. "Didn't anyone wonder why I was in your car and not my truck?"

Everyone just looked at him, waiting for another story. "I walked back to my neighborhood from here. But my neighborhood wasn't there. My trailer and my truck were wiped out, along with everything. All I have are these clothes I'm wearing. Some kind of large vehicle went through there. People around there said it was a large jet. I don't even have a job because the store was wiped out too."

"I was wondering," said Lori. "Could Ken and I have Grandma and Grandpa's house since they don't need it anymore?"

"Are you kidding?" said Josh. "At least you have a place to live. I need to move in there."

"Maybe I can move in with you, Josh," said Larry. "I don't want to live alone without Sydney."

A big argument broke out, but Matt interrupted. "Ken, you guys could move into your mom's house, right?"

"Actually my mom's house is a little crowded now,"

said Ken. "My sister Marin and her two kids have lived there for a while. But now, my sister Susan, her husband, and their three kids just moved in too. A large delivery truck went through their house when the driver disappeared. It will take a while to get it fixed up enough to live in."

"We can keep renting if we have to," said Lori. "But maybe if Josh gets their house, Ken and I could have Grandma and Grandpa's car. Then one of us can get a better job and we can get out of this rut we're in."

"That could work," said Matt. "But I have another idea. Do you guys think your minivan could make a two-hour trip?"

"Maybe," said Ken. "Where are we going?"

"I need to let my sister Melinda know about Grandma and Grandpa and Sydney," said Matt. "But she didn't answer the phone. I left a message for her to call me back, and I left messages with their four married kids." Matt looked over at his answering machine. "As you can see, the machine is not blinking. They could all be missing."

"The whole family?" asked Lori. "They have seven kids, some with spouses and children of their own. What are the odds that everyone in their family disappeared?"

"Well, we need to check it out," said Matt. "And if they all left the planet, we could go through their stuff. They might even have a few vehicles they don't need anymore."

"I could seriously go for a road trip," said Lori. "But what if we get called in to work tomorrow?"

"Let me think," said Ken. "If we don't answer the phone, they will assume we disappeared or got injured out on the roads. When we get back, we'll make up something."

"What about you Rosemary? Are you up to a trip to Canton, Ohio?" asked Matt.

"After a good night's sleep, I should be fine to ride in the car," she answered. "But could we just go into their house and take what we want?"

"Let's find out about them. If no one shows up, their house and everything in it could be ours," said Matt. "If we don't go tomorrow, the neighbors might get the same idea."

"I can go too," said Josh.

"Hold on Josh," said Matt. "Did you even lock up Grandma and Grandpa's house? And what about their cats? If you want their place you should go and take care of it."

"Wait Dad, this is important," said Josh, almost crying. "We lost family members. We need to stay together, for comfort. I'll run over to their house. I'll give the cats lots of food and water, and fresh kitty litter. I'll lock up their house real tight. When you get up in the morning, I'll be right here, sleeping in the recliner, and ready to go."

"Can I go too?" asked Larry. "I can't stay alone right now."

"I guess you can both go," said Matt.

Just then the phone rang. They all looked at each other, holding their breath.

"I wish I would have paid for caller ID," said Matt. He walked over and answered the phone. He listened for a minute and then said, "Hold on." Matt put his hand over the mouthpiece and spoke very quietly.

"It's Allison," said Matt, looking at Josh.

"Don't tell her anything!" Josh whispered.

"No one has seen him," said Matt. "But I'll tell him

you called if he comes around." He hung up and said, "Why did I lie? I hate lying."

Josh was furious. "She probably wants my stuff so she can sell it and buy booze."

"She saw your neighborhood on the news and wanted to know if you are alright," said Matt.

"Well, she never really cared before," said Josh. His face was red and he had tears in his eyes. "I'm over her. Now let's plan our trip. What time do you want us all here in the morning?"

"Wait a minute," said Matt. "What about your family Larry?"

"Oh they're alright," said Larry. "No one disappeared and they were home, safe and sound. They weren't worried about me, because they knew I was with you guys."

Matt smiled. "That settles it then. We're all going. Lori and Ken. You two get plenty of gas. And all of you gather any cash you can find, especially around Grandma and Grandpa's house. Oh, and eat breakfast, because we won't stop and eat. Hopefully we can get something at Melinda's house. Pack a little bag, and be here ready to leave at 9am sharp."

Everyone took off. Josh and Larry both said they will be back as soon as possible and sleep in the living room. Matt helped Rosemary to bed. He made her a hot chocolate to help her sleep, but she was already asleep when he took it to her. Matt drank it himself. He was excited about their little adventure. Even though he was sad about his parents, and of course Sydney, he had a feeling that things were going to turn around for them.

CHAPTER THREE

Wednesday, Day Two

The next morning went exactly the way they planned it. Josh was on the sofa, and Larry was in the recliner. Rosemary was feeling surprisingly energetic. Matt got each of them into the shower when he was finished. Lori and Ken pulled up right on time and everyone loaded a small travel bag or backpack into the van.

The trip to Jack and Melinda's house was very interesting. The first hour of the trip was fine. There were a few cars that had crashed into trees and telephone poles, but they didn't bother to stop since any stranded passengers would have been found by now. Then they came across a real problem- a derailed train that blocked the road. What could have happened? They had to turn around.

"Did anyone remember to bring a map?" asked Ken.

"No. Let's try turning right," suggested Lori. They retraced the path, and then turned right at the first side road. They traveled about 15 minutes, and the road seemed to be curving to the right. Maybe they wouldn't be set back much time at all. Then they saw a sight they couldn't believe. A huge 18-wheeler had crashed through a railroad crossing. The immense truck was on its side, with a train sprawled over and around it. Even though the accident probably happened yesterday around 2:15 pm, there was smoke coming from the crash site, and firemen were still looking for survivors.

"It's going to be a while before they clean up this mess. We have no choice but to go back again and try to find another northbound road," said Ken. Most of the family could care less how they get there. Ken went back to the crossroads, and this time he went left and found a northbound road that wasn't blocked off. Eventually they arrived in the city and came to Jack and Melinda's home.

They sat in the driveway for quite a while, looking at the house. There was a Ford Explorer out front. Rosemary asked, "Who do you think that Explorer belongs to?"

Lori always tried to keep track of her cousins, so she answered. "It's probably Jamie's car. He's still living at home, and I think he's a senior at Malone College."

The family finally got the nerve to get out of the car. They went up and knocked on the door. They rang the doorbell. No one answered. Finally Matt tried the front door, and it wasn't even locked. They all walked in and looked around. Ken called out, "Is anybody home?" He raced upstairs and checked all of the rooms. Then he checked the main level and the basement. "I'm pretty sure no one is here. This is one big house."

When Ken came back, he found the family standing around a pile in the living room. Lori had a theory. "Someone must have just gotten the mail. He or she must have been carrying it in when taken. That's why it's scattered all over the floor."

Everyone walked into the kitchen. "Look, the microwave says 'End,' and I bet there is an afterschool snack in there," said Ken. He opened the door and there was a popped bag of popcorn. Over by the back door near the garage was a huge backpack and a jacket. "What do you do when you get home from school? Go to the bathroom, get a drink, check the mail, and make popcorn. It was probably Jesse. He's in high school, right?"

"You mean that he was in high school. I don't think he will see his graduation day," said Lori. "This is really sad."

Larry went upstairs and was snooping around. He came to a room with a computer that was still on and a CD player that was still playing. Someone must have set it to play over and over. A half-eaten granola bar lay next to the computer mouse, and a half-drank glass of milk was next to that.

Larry ran down the steps. "Hey, everyone. I think I know what happened to the college guy. What's his name?"

"Jamie," they all said.

"Well, now we know he disappeared. Nobody leaves a glass of milk in their room. After a while it smells bad," said Larry. "I did that once and never again."

Suddenly there was a knock at the door. They opened it and most of the family recognized a girl from family weddings. She was crying.

"Hi. Remember me? I'm Brook from next door. I left a message for them to call me, and I left a message for Amy to call me. She's my best friend, you know. Neither one called me," said Brook. "Do you think they disappeared?"

"We think so. We left messages too," said Matt. "We

just decided to get in the car and see for ourselves. How about you? Did you lose anyone?"

"My mom and I were walking into the grocery store together. Suddenly I was walking alone. I still can't believe it happened," said Brook. "I talked to my dad. He and my step-mom are fine. I haven't heard from my sister and her husband. They are nurses in Columbus. I figure they are tied up in the hospital since so many are injured. Hopefully they will call me soon."

"I'm sure you're right," said Lori. "We were at a hospital down there yesterday. There were patients all over the emergency room, and they had everyone working that they could get ahold of. I'm sorry to hear about your mom. Any idea where they all went?"

"No," said Brook. "It's the strangest thing I ever heard of. And why mom? She was so nice to everyone."

"Grandma and Grandpa were too," said Lori. "And Sydney wasn't perfect, but she never hurt anyone, so why her?"

"We may never know why or where they went," said Brook. "But would you like to go to Melinda's school with me? I sub there. They might be able to tell us what happened to her."

"I want to go there," said Matt. "Anyone else want to go to Melinda's school and find out what happened to her?"

"Not me," said Rosemary. "I think I'll just poke around the yard and stretch my legs after all that riding in the car."

"I'll go Dad," said Lori. "I would love to see where Aunt Melinda worked. Maybe she's still there."

They drove the pleasant twenty minute drive to

Lehman Middle School. Matt told Brook about the mail on the floor and their conclusion that Jesse disappeared just after school with popcorn in the microwave. He also told her about the milk and the granola bar next to the computer in that upstairs bedroom. Brook agreed that Jesse and Jamie probably both disappeared.

"Don't they have another girl in the family who isn't married yet?" asked Matt.

"Stephanie," said Lori.

"Yes," said Brook. "Stephanie goes to an out-of-state Christian college. I can't think of the name of it."

The three of them arrived at the middle school around lunch time. Brook was surprised that the secretary wasn't in the office.

"I'm Naomi. I'm filling in for Carolyn who is not here. What can I do for you?"

"What happened to Carolyn," asked Brook. "Did she disappear?"

"I'm sorry to say she did," said Naomi. "We lost one principal, six staff members, and fifty students."

"Well I'm Brook Morrison and I sub here. I was surprised they didn't call me in today," said Brook.

"We had plenty of subs for today, but if you want a long-term job, fill out one of these applications," said Naomi.

"Oh thank you," said Brook. "This is Melinda Walker's brother and her niece. We were just hoping to find out what happened to Melinda."

A teacher came around the corner from the copy room. She said, "I couldn't help hearing your conversation. I was here yesterday when people disappeared. I talked to a couple of students who were very upset when they saw

Melinda disappear right before their eyes. I saw those girls today and they are still upset. Of course, they probably lost family members too. Most of us did."

Another teacher came into the office and was introduced to Matt, Lori, and Brook. She asked if they would like Melinda's purse.

"Yes," Matt answered. "We'll take any of her personal effects. Did she have a car?"

"Oh, of course," said the teacher. She led them into Melinda's room, pulled the keys out of Melinda's purse, and handed them to Matt, along with the purse. Then she led them to the window of the classroom and pointed out Melinda's car. Then she just started crying. "I'm sorry," she said. "I've done this a lot today. I just start crying. I don't know if I'm sad about the ones who disappeared, or if I'm scared that I'll be next."

"Do you think more people are going to be taken?" asked Brook. "Why didn't I think of that?"

"I think the rest of us are safe," said Matt. "I'm not going to worry about it anyway."

Matt and the girls walked to the car. "Thank you so much Brook for bringing us here to find out what happened to Aunt Melinda," said Lori. "It's just better to know."

Matt clicked the door unlock button for Melinda's car, and asked, "Lori, are you riding with me?"

"No, I think I'll ride home with Brook," said Lori. "Maybe we can figure out what her mom had in common with Grandma and Grandpa and Sydney. If we know why they were taken we might not have to worry about more people disappearing."

"Sounds good," said Brook. "I don't want to worry about disappearing."

Matt got into Melinda's blue Taurus and followed the girls home. *Why would Mom and Dad and Sydney disappear? And why Melinda and her family? And where are they now?* Matt wondered.

CHAPTER FOUR

When Matt and Lori arrived at the house, the place smelled wonderful. Rosemary, Josh, Ken, and Larry made dinner. "Wow, did they have all this food in the refrigerator?" asked Lori.

"We can eat here for two weeks without even going to the store," said Ken.

Matt and Lori told the family about Melinda disappearing right in front of her students.

"Just like Sydney," said Rosemary. "She was there and then suddenly, she wasn't there.

"Probably Grandma and Grandpa too," said Josh. "I should have seen it, but I was sound asleep."

The phone rang for the first time since they arrived. "I wondered why nobody calls them," said Matt.

Matt went to the phone and answered it. "Hello," he said.

The person on the phone sounded very loud and excited. "Please slow down," Matt said. "I can't follow you."

He listened quietly and finally said, "Well, I'm her uncle. That will be fine. Just make sure you get your family to help bring it here as soon as you get in."

"What?" asked Matt. "Oh, I'm sure you'll find someone around. Drive carefully." He hung up and looked at the curious family.

"Well we were wondering about Stephanie, and now we know," said Matt. "She was away at Kentucky Christian University. According to the girl on the phone, Stephanie was in a classroom where every student disappeared except one guy, and he told this girl, Rachel, all about it. Anyway this girl is scared and lonely. She said the college no longer exists and there are only a few students left on campus. She says that no one answers when she calls home, and that her family hasn't even called and asked about her. Anyway, she's driving Stephanie's car home, because she doesn't have a car. Her family lives about ten minutes from here."

"That phone call reminded me of something," said Rosemary. "There were some interesting messages on their answering machine. There were calls from both of Jack's sisters wanting to know if he's alright. We should use their caller ID and call them back, or they will come here and check on him. Also there was a strange message from Jesse's school principal. What do you think that was about?"

"Oh they probably just want to know if he's coming back to school," said Josh.

The family ate a quiet dinner. They were all a little shaken up from the phone call from the college girl. Josh turned on the TV to watch the news. There was surprisingly little news about the disappearances. Then the governor of the state came on to warn about looting. He said that all possessions were to remain within the family, and that care must be taken to keep up payments on purchased items, such as cars, boats, houses, etc. The governor also said that in cases where the whole family disappeared, the property will be owned by the state.

"Well, we're family," said Matt. "How are we supposed to know if they were making payments on anything?"

"We will just have to go through their checkbooks and bills," said Lori.

"Maybe we could sell this house," said Rosemary. "We could buy something better back home."

"I was thinking that maybe we could just stay here," said Matt. "Maybe we could sell Jack's business and live off that for a couple of years."

They cleaned up the kitchen in no time. "What do you want to do now?" asked Lori. "Do you want to watch a movie?"

"First," said Rosemary, "we need to know where we are sleeping tonight. Matt and I get the big room upstairs. It must be Jack and Melinda's room."

"We get the room with the red carpet on the first floor," said Lori. "It's such a pretty room."

Larry laughed and said, "I feel like the three bears. We ate their porridge and sat in their chairs. Now we are going to sleep in their beds. I hope we don't wake up in the morning with them shouting at us."

"I hope we do wake up and they're back, because that would mean Sydney is back," said Rosemary.

"Where do you want to sleep, Larry?" asked Lori.

"I'll take the upstairs room with the computer and books and TV," said Larry.

"That's Jamie's room," said Ken. "He does have a nice set up. It's like a small apartment. Did anyone dump his milk?"

"I took care of that," said Rosemary. "Do you know they don't have any alcohol in this house?"

Josh wondered, "Aren't they a little on the boring side? Is that why you never wanted to visit them?"

"I stayed away because I didn't want them preaching to me to go to church," said Matt. "I gave that up a long time ago. Look where church got them. Lost. Missing. Vanished. I'm glad I'm still here."

Everyone went off to bed. There were more bedrooms, but Josh threw himself down on a couch in the family room and started flipping channels. Many of the stations had returned to regular programing. One talk show was discussing theories about what caused the disappearances. The most popular theory was the one that aliens from a faraway planet kidnapped the people to help repopulate after a catastrophic event. Josh just shook his head. There has to be a more reasonable explanation than that.

Upstairs, Matt was tossing and turning. He just remembered that Sydney surely had insurance on their car. Maybe Larry can get money for the totaled car and get himself another one. Then he remembered that Jack probably had a car. First thing tomorrow, he was going to find Jack's store. Matt drifted off to sleep thinking that if he played his cards right, he might never have to return to that horrible job back home.

At 3:00 am, the family woke up to intense banging on the front door. Matt and Rosemary were shaking all over. Had the police come to arrest them for being here? Maybe one of Jack and Melinda's married kids was here. He looked out an upstairs window. There was a car in the driveway, but he couldn't see who was banging on the door. He swallowed hard, looked back at a terrified Rosemary, and went downstairs. He turned on the outside light and peeked out the window near the front door. It was a girl. He opened the door and let her in.

The girl was a mess, crying and talking very rapidly. "I'm Rachel. I called a few hours ago. Remember, I drove Stephanie's car home from college. You said it was alright, didn't you?"

"Oh, that's right," said Matt. "Why are you so upset?"

"I tried to tell you," said Rachel. "I stopped off at my house. My parents weren't there and the front door was unlocked. The place is a mess. Things are missing. We've been robbed! For all I know the robbers might still be in the house. I ran back to the car and came straight here. Please, can I stay here tonight with you guys? Just tonight."

"Oh, I guess you can stay," said Matt. "It's not our house anyway."

"Are you hungry?" asked Lori.

"I'm starving," said Rachel. "I haven't eaten anything since yesterday at lunch. I went through some of the girls' purses in my dorm looking for money. I mean, they aren't going to use it. But I didn't get enough. I used it all for gas."

Lori led Rachel into the kitchen and had her sit on a stool. Then she warmed up leftovers from dinner as Ken got her a drink.

"How many girls were left in your dorm and were they all rummaging for money and car keys?" asked Ken.

"I searched the whole dorm," said Rachel. "I was the only one there. I had some friends in other dorms and apartments who were still around. They were rebels like me. You know, bad kids sent there by our parents to get us straightened out. It didn't work. Anyway, they left and didn't even offer me a ride."

Rachel ate for a while and then laid her head down on the counter.

"Come on," said Lori. "I have a room for you, just around the corner." She led her into a room with a full bed, bunk beds, and a crib. "Take your pick Rachel. I'll run and get you a towel and washcloth. Look, you even have your own little half bath. You're safe now. Have a good sleep."

Lori ran around the house and put towels and washcloths outside everyone's bedroom. She even dropped one next to a sleeping Josh. She thought to herself, *I could get used to this place.*

When Lori and Ken got to their room, they talked in a whisper. "You want to make a wager?" asked Ken.

"What about?" asked Lori.

"Did you see the tattoo on that girl? Well, she can't do anything about that. But I'll bet that lip ring and eyebrow thing will be gone in two days," Ken said.

"Why should she get rid of them?" asked Lori. "She probably likes them."

"The point is," said Ken, "there is no one around for her to rebel against. None of us are going to make her go to church. We don't care what she looks like. With no one around to rebel against, she will lose those things that are uncomfortable. You'll see."

"What makes you think that she will be here in two days? We might not be here in two days," said Lori.

"She obviously doesn't have a friend in the world. She doesn't even know us, but we're all she's got right now. As for us, I'm just not ready to go back to that dead-end life we were living. I won't miss the job, our friends, or even our apartment. How about you?" asked Ken.

"You're right," Lori said. "We can't miss our life, because we weren't really living."

CHAPTER FIVE

Thursday, Day Three

All Matt had to do to find Jack's pharmacy was look it up in the phone book. After breakfast he asked, "Who wants to go with me to find Jack's store?" Josh, Ken, and Larry all wanted to go along, so they piled into Melinda's car. The tank was almost empty, so they pulled into a station. Matt flashed a gas card in the air and said, "This fill-up is on Melinda."

Josh had a bad feeling about that. Staying in their house was fine, but using their credit cards after they disappeared seemed like asking for trouble. He looked at Ken to see if he felt the same way, and Ken just shrugged. Matt had no trouble paying with the card at the pump, so they were soon on their way.

The four men pulled into the pharmacy parking lot. There weren't any cars there, but there was a sign posted on the door. They all jumped out of the car and went to the door and peeked in. The sign on the door read, "Jack, Debbie, and Jane all went to be with the Lord at 2:17 pm on Tuesday, and their disappearance was witnessed by Earl and Wilma James. Feel free to call with any questions.

A police car went by, so they went to the car to call the number.

Matt had one of Melinda's boy's cell phones. He listened quietly and then said, "The old folks live just around the corner, and they have Jack's van, or maybe I should say, my van."

"What about this car?" asked Ken.

"I thought Rosemary would enjoy having a car of her own for once in her life," said Matt.

"Oh come on," said Josh. "Mom will never get a license. You know that."

"Please," said Ken. "Could Lori and I have Melinda's car? Then one of us could get a better job, and we won't have to work at the same place."

"We'll talk about it," said Matt. "We may even sell it. We could use some cash to live on."

They pulled into Earl and Wilma's driveway, who had a charming little house with a perfectly landscaped yard. Earl came to the door and invited them in. He and Wilma treated them like long, lost friends.

"Can you tell us what happened to Jack?" Matt asked.

"We were there when he disappeared," Earl said. "Jack was handing me a bag with my medicine in it, and suddenly, he was gone. It was so shocking. We couldn't believe our eyes. Two of the ladies working there disappeared too. And I wasn't about to go off and leave Jack's business unprotected, so we found the keys and called the security company and locked it up tight."

"Thank you for that," said Matt. "Did you write the note that's on the front door of the pharmacy?"

Earl nodded his head and smiled.

"Why did you write that Jack, Debbie, and Jane went to be with the Lord?" asked Matt. "How could you possibly reach such a conclusion?"

Earl and Wilma looked at each other. Wilma got tears in her eyes, and Earl patted her hand, comforting her. "Our granddaughter Amanda was a very dedicated and enthusiastic Christian," said Wilma. "Her faith was the most important thing in her life. Don't get me wrong. She was a terrific wife and mother, and she was so kind to Wilma and me."

"Amanda was at that church all the time," said Earl. "And she tried to warn us about the Rapture. She said that Jesus Christ was going to come someday soon and take his followers to heaven with him and that non-believers would be left here on earth. We thought she was a fanatic and we told her to stop talking about it. So she did."

"I guess our daughter Linda and her husband listened to Amanda because they seem to be gone too," said Wilma. "We're left all alone now." Wilma dabbed her eyes with a tissue.

"Well, your story makes a lot of sense," said Matt. "Everyone we know who disappeared were Christians too. And just like you folks, we didn't want to hear about it."

"Yeah, we barely knew our cousins, because Mom and Dad didn't want them telling us to go to church," said Josh.

"When I graduated from high school, my friend and I decided we weren't going to church anymore," said Matt. "I don't know about my friend, but I never went back to church. Rosemary and I had our wedding in the back yard."

"All I know," said Josh, "is that kids should spend

time with their cousins, and we barely ever got to."

"Why did you quit going to church?" asked Wilma.

"I don't know," said Matt. "It just seemed so boring. I had other things I wanted to do. I would have quit sooner, but Mom and Dad made me go until I graduated."

"Grandma and Grandpa took us a lot, but Sydney was the only one who kept going," said Josh. "She tried to get Lori and me to go, but we wouldn't."

"Well I wish I would have gone with her," said Larry. "Then we would still be together."

"We wish we would have listened too," said Earl. "But we are reading the Bible now and hoping we get a second chance. You should start reading it too. We don't know what the future holds, but it's better to be on God's side than away from him."

"Well, we will think about it," said Matt. "Now did you say something about having Jack's keys?"

"Yes," said Earl. "Here are the keys to the van. I took them off the keychain for you."

"Why did you do that?" Matt asked. "Are you planning to do something with the store?"

"Oh, no," said Earl. "There is a law that only a pharmacist can go in there. We can't even open the doors. You may be able to sell the place, but only a pharmacist can go in. My neighbor told me all this. She works for a pharmacy."

They shook hands with Earl and Wilma and headed for the cars.

"Do you want me to drive the car home?" asked Ken.

Matt threw him the keys. Matt and Josh got in the van, and Larry got in the car with Ken. It was a twenty-five minute drive back to Jack and Melinda's house. Matt was silent all the way, thinking about his childhood and his church. He remembered going to Vacation Bible School. It was always at night, because most of the members were farmers, who could only help at night. He remembered marching into the church while the pianist played "Onward Christian Soldiers." He remembered listening to the Bible stories and making crafts out of Popsicle sticks, and he remembered eating the neatest snacks. After VBS, the children ran and played outside around the church building until their parents had cleaned up their space and were ready to drive home. Matt remembered riding home with the warm summer air blowing his hair and the lightning bugs blinking everywhere. Those were good times. When he got older, he stopped listening. The preacher seemed boring. He just wanted to go home, put on his comfortable clothes, and go hang out with his friends.

Melinda was different. She started helping with the little kids. She sat and cut out little sheep and fish and things, and she loved helping in the toddler class. When she was in college, she was very homesick. Instead of coming home more often, she read her Bible all the time. She said it really got her through the lonely times.

Matt thought he might try reading Melinda's Bible tonight at bedtime. Rosemary will probably make fun of him. He decided to wait until she falls asleep.

Josh interrupted his thoughts. "Dad, don't you think we should call Uncle Jack's sisters and tell them what happened to him? I listened to their messages and they sounded so worried. If we don't call them and let them know what happened to him, they might come here to find out.

"I never thought of that Son," said Matt. "I'll call one sister, and she can call the rest of their family. We don't have to tell them we are taking the cars. What they don't know won't hurt them.

"Will there be a car for me, Dad?" asked Josh.

"Of course," said Matt. "You can have Jamie's Explorer. It's a little old, but it will get you around."

"I think I can handle that, but he probably has a car payment, even on a used car," said Josh. "Do you think I can handle that?"

"Time will tell Josh. Time will tell," said Matt. He was silent for the rest of the trip home, trying to remember why he was so determined to stay away from church back then.

CHAPTER SIX

When Matt and Josh got home, Rosemary came out to check out their new van. Matt told her about the possibility of selling the pharmacy, but he didn't tell her about Earl and Wilma's theory that the Lord came and took all those people to heaven.

Lori and Rachel made lunch this time. Ken and Larry walked in, and Ken looked at Lori and smiled. Sure enough, Rachel had already removed the lip ring and the thing in her eyebrow. She looked a lot more relaxed than she did last night. After they ate lunch, Matt went to the phone, checked out the Caller ID, and figured out the number to call Jack's sister.

Matt dialed the number, and it rang a few times and someone answered. "Jack dear, is that you? I've been so worried."

"No, I'm sorry. This is Matt Moses, Melinda's brother. We were so worried about Jack and Melinda that we drove up yesterday to find out what happened to them. Are you Jack's sister? I only had the recorded message to go on."

"Yes, I'm Jack's sister, Margaret," she answered. "Do you know anything about them?"

"From the evidence we've gathered, we are fairly certain that Jack, Melinda, Jamie, Stephanie, and Jesse all disappeared. Their four married children are probably gone too, since they haven't called and they don't answer their phones," said Matt.

"Well, thanks for checking on them," Margaret said. "We've lost some of our own children and grandchildren."

"I'm so sorry for your loss," said Matt. "Will you let the rest of your family know about Jack and Melinda and their family?"

"I certainly will. I wish we were talking under happier circumstances. Will you give us a call sometime, so we can keep in touch?" asked Margaret.

Matt said he would, but he thought to himself, *in your dreams*!

The family all sat down in the family room together. They were all in good spirits because it seemed to them very unlikely that any of Jack's side of the family will come snooping around. Everything here, the house, the business, the cars, the computers, books, movies, games, etc. belonged to them.

They decided to watch TV. An ad for Disney World came on. The park was offering special packages to encourage business and they were teaming up with Delta Airlines, the only major airline that suffered no crashes on Tuesday.

Rachel, their visitor, spoke up. "I always wanted to go to Disney World. My parents never took me. They took my brother and sister before I was born. I always resented it."

"Are your brother and sister missing?" asked Ken.

"I guess they are, and my parents too," said Rachel.

"They never called to see if I was OK. I'm not sure they would though. I've been pretty bad for several years."

"Well I like you," said Josh. "Next to my old girlfriend, you're a saint."

"I never got to go to Disney World either said Larry. "All my friends went. I even got invited to go with my friend Zach and his family once. My mom and dad said I couldn't go. Zach's family offered to pay all my expenses, but they wouldn't let me go. They treated all three of us kids like that- like we didn't deserve anything nice."

"How about you, Ken?" asked Matt. "Did you ever go to Disney World?"

"My parents took me and the girls once, but I don't remember it," Ken answered. "I guess I was pretty young."

"We went a few years ago," said Matt, "but I think we should go and take Rachel, Larry, and Ken."

Rachel was astonished. "You barely know me. Are you sure you want to take me?"

Matt got tears in his eyes. "You lost your family, and we lost our girl. If you want to go with us, you're welcome. What do you say everybody? Shall we see if Jack and Melinda have enough money for us to go on a nice trip? And remember, it is a bargain."

Larry was so excited that he jumped to his feet. "Did you catch that website? Jamie's computer is still turned on to that paper he was writing, so I bet we can use the internet."

"We can find it," said Lori. "Let's go check it out."

"I'll come up too," said Matt, "and bring Melinda's credit card to make the reservations. How many of us are there anyway?"

Lori looked around. "Let's see. There's Dad, Mom,

me, and Ken. That's four. Josh, Larry, and Rachel bring the total to seven. Do you think we can get by with two rooms? Ken and I can share with you and Mom," she said.

Josh and Larry looked at Rachel. They looked embarrassed.

"Hey, I'm your new sister," said Rachel. "I'll sleep on the couch."

"Most motel rooms have two queen-sized beds," said Matt. "Rachel, you can have your own bed and Josh and Larry can share the other one. Maybe we can get adjoining rooms."

"Yeah, that's fine," said Rachel. Josh and Larry nodded in agreement.

Lori asked, "Rachel, what's your last name, for the reservation?"

Rachel said, "My name is Rachel McGovern."

"You all need to bring your drivers' license," said Lori. "Or a photo ID for you Mom."

Rachel's biggest worry was her wardrobe. Her clothes were pretty far-out. She didn't know why, but now she wasn't comfortable in those clothes anymore.

It was as if Lori could read her mind. "Jack and Melinda had three daughters. After we make reservations, we can go clothes shopping, right here in the house."

Rosemary spoke up for the first time since the subject of the trip came up. "I can look through the girls' clothes too. I still wear junior sizes."

"You sure can," said Matt. "Have fun."

First they made plane reservations for seven, and they decided to go for seven days.

"I know tomorrow is kind of sudden," said Matt. "Right now, it seems fine to spend Jack and Melinda's money, since we are close relatives. But the government might freeze the money of everyone who disappeared. Let's enjoy it while we can."

The family got wonderful deals on plane tickets, hotels, and tickets to Disney World. There was even a free shuttle every day from the hotel to the parks, and then back to the airport in seven days.

Ken suggested that they all need spending money on the trip, especially for food. "Why don't we all divide up and search for purses, wallets, and piggy banks around the house?" Ken said. "While the girls are looking for clothes, we guys can look for cash."

Jamie's billfold was right there in his room. They pulled a whole $7.00 out of it. There was a debit card there too, and Ken put it in his pocket. Then he searched two other upstairs bedrooms. Altogether he found $94. He frowned. That was not enough. Lori came running up the stairs and twirled around in a new outfit.

"What do you think?" Lori asked.

"Very nice," Ken answered. "Do you have any money?"

"I sure do," said Lori. "I was saving to buy you an X-Box for your birthday. Now you can just take Jamie's. I think I have around $300 in my account. We can use my debit card." Ken added that in with what he had collected and figured that if they were careful, it would be enough money for their vacation.

"Well pack your bag, Ken," said Lori. "If you need more clothes, check out Jamie and Jesse's closets."

"Their clothes are too small for me," said Ken. "Besides, I never unpacked. I'm ready to go."

Matt came down the stairs, and he had a big smile

on his face. "Guess what kids. I found an envelope in Jack's drawer with $750 in it. It was labeled 'Mission trip to Haiti.' Well they won't be making that trip, so I'm sure they would want us to use it for our trip. Rosemary and I can get by on part of that. Who else needs money?"

Josh said, "I'm good Dad. Once I split up with Allison, I noticed that I don't need much money to live on. Anyway, I can pay for my own food. I don't eat that much."

Matt asked Josh, "That reminds me of your friend Eddie who let you use his trailer. Have you talked to him lately?"

Josh looked kind of sad. "That night when I discovered that my neighborhood was missing, I ran into Eddie's girlfriend," Josh said. "She said that Eddie disappeared along with his mom, dad, and grandparents. They were all eating out together, because they were going to announce their engagement. She showed me her ring and then she started crying. Actually, I was thinking about calling her."

"You would go out with your best friend's fiancé?" asked Larry.

"No," said Josh. "I was just going to call her and ask if she likes cats. I thought maybe she could take Grandma and Grandpa's cats, or at least feed them while we are gone. Did you forget about their cats? I didn't!"

"Good thinking, Josh," said Matt. "I did forget about the cats in all the commotion. Now what were we talking about?"

"Money," said Larry. "Actually, I could use some food money for our trip. I have no idea how much money I have. Sydney took care of all that. I'm going to have to learn all about that stuff."

Lori walked into the room just then. "Larry, don't you have a debit card in your wallet?" she asked.

Larry opened his wallet and sure enough, next to his driver's license was a debit card. "I never used this before. I forgot I had one."

"Larry, you use your own debit card," said Matt. "It's very easy. Now, do you have any money Rachel?"

"Not that I can get my hands on," said Rachel. "I have an account at school, but there is no way to get that money out. But I can look around my house and see if the robbers missed some, if someone will go with me."

"Well here is $200 for food. You'll have to be careful," said Matt. "If you run out, we can try some of the cards we gathered up around the house."

"Well, I'm all packed and ready to go," said Rosemary. "Now I'm going to get dinner." She eyed Rachel's black leather-look outfit. "Don't you want to look through the girl's clothes? You'll be kind of hot in Florida in that outfit."

"I feel kind of funny getting into their closets," said Rachel. "I knew Stephanie but we weren't very close."

Rosemary laughed. "She won't be needing her clothes now, will she? Get yourself a bag and find some clothes while I start cooking."

"Come on, Rachel, I'll help," said Lori. The two of them went upstairs.

"Are you boys packed?" Matt asked, looking at Josh and Larry.

"I'm fine," said Larry. "I have an extra pair of jeans, three T-shirts, and lots of clean underwear. Plus I have my bathroom supplies. What more do I need?" He patted a very stuffed backpack.

"Good," said Matt. "What about you, Josh?"

"What I'm wearing is all I have," said Josh. "My cousins' clothes are too big for me. I'll run over to the store after dinner and get a few things."

Ken and Larry helped Rosemary get dinner just like when they first arrived. They made a big pan of stir fry. The delicious aroma brought everyone to the kitchen. Lori and Rachel came into the room. Rachel had a cute suitcase with wheels on it and a new wardrobe inside. Lori had even given her a cute haircut. Rachel looked so happy.

"I just want to thank you all so much for taking me in and treating me like family," Rachel said.

As the family ate their meal, Matt asked, "Josh, any luck with the cats?"

"No, Eddie's girlfriend just got offered her first teaching job," said Josh. "She's in a panic to plan her first day. No time for cats!"

"I'll call the Snyder family and tell them where the key is," said Matt. "I never liked them much, but they do live in town a couple blocks from Mom and Dad's house."

After dinner everyone had a job to do. Matt called the Snyder family, who agreed to feed and care for his parents' cats. Rosemary asked Brook to keep an eye on the house and report if anyone tried to break in while they were away. Josh and Larry took the Explorer and went to get a few clothes for Josh. Lori and Ken took Rachel over to her house to check out the place and see if there was anything left that they could use, especially cash. Later, they were all back in the family room, packed and ready for bed.

"Do you all want to watch the news?" asked Ken.

"No," answered several of them. They couldn't take

any more people crying for missing family members. It was depressing and it reminded them of their own losses.

Matt asked Josh if he found any clothes. "Yes, I did," Josh answered. "I got a pair of jeans, a pair of shorts, four T-shirts, ten pair of underwear, and these boxers to sleep in."

He stood up and modeled the boxers and matching T-shirt and everyone went, "Woo- woo."

"We had an interesting visit to Rachel's house," said Ken.

"Yes," spoke Rachel. "I found my mom's purse in the file cabinet. I remembered that she always kept it there. She had $45 in there plus a debit card. I'm pretty sure she was sitting at the table reading her Bible when she disappeared. She had a tea sitting there and a prayer journal. I looked back through the pages, and I was the first on her prayer list every day. She never gave up on me." Rachel started crying.

"Her dad must have been home too. His billfold was in his pants pocket, on the bed," said Lori. "We found $85 inside and a cute picture of Rachel."

"When I was about twelve," said Rachel.

Ken described the rest of the visit. "We cleaned up the mess made by the crooks," he said, "and we locked up the place. We had to bring in the lawn mower. We think Rachel's dad was mowing when he disappeared, since the mower was out in the yard and the garage door was left open."

"I guess I can have my mom and dad's cars if I want them," said Rachel. "They were both in the garage. I have both sets of keys, so if there are any more intruders, they won't be able to take the cars."

"Did you find anything helpful besides money?" asked Josh.

"Yes," answered Rachel. "I have my mom's Bible, her prayer journal, and her wrap-up. It still smells good like her."

CHAPTER SEVEN

Friday, Day Four

The family went to bed, and the next morning they all piled into Lori and Ken's car. They arrived at the airport with plenty of time to spare, checked in, and got their tickets. They boarded the plane, and they were a little surprised that there weren't more people on the plane with them. The flight went well without any incident. Rachel read her mother's Bible the entire time. Matt was reading Melinda's Bible too, and he quit worrying about what anyone thought. As their jet landed, they couldn't help but notice that the sky was getting dark to the southwest. Thick, dark clouds were rolling in.

The Orlando Airport was nothing like the calm airport up north. People were jammed in like cattle, waiting for flights out, and they were anything but calm. There was some yelling and pushing. By the time they got to their shuttle, the wind was gusting and it started raining.

"Looks like a storm is coming," said Matt to the shuttle driver.

"What, are you kidding?" asked the driver. "Haven't you heard about the hurricane? Don't you ever watch the news? This is the last run I'm making."

"How long is it going to last?" Matt asked the driver.

"Who knows?" said the driver. "They are saying this is the biggest storm recorded in history. It covers the entire Gulf of Mexico, and it has been sitting there for the last two days getting fueled by the warm gulf waters. As you can see, here it comes."

"How far are we from the All-Star Resort?" asked Josh.

"I'm sorry to tell you that you aren't going there," said the driver. "But you are very fortunate to have reservations at a Disney resort. That's because my boss, the hotel owner, is taking you in, along with five other families that were checking in to other hotels. Most people in the state of Florida are trying to get out of here one way or another."

Everyone was silent for the next twenty minutes as they traveled to some unknown hotel. They couldn't talk if they wanted to because of the roar of the storm. Debris was hitting the windows and making everyone quite nervous.

"Where are you going after dropping us off?" yelled Matt.

"Same place as you," he answered. "My whole family is already there. I have a wife and three teenagers." He probably would have talked more, but he needed to concentrate fully on his driving.

Fortunately, they arrived safely, as the driver went into an underground parking area. Everyone was relieved. Matt gave the shuttle driver a good tip for getting them there alive. The family grabbed their bags and climbed the stairs to the lobby, which was boarded up. They met a nice-looking man in casual clothes at the check-in desk.

He reached out his hand and shook Matt's and asked, "Are you the Moses family?" They nodded yes, and he continued. "I'm William Gardner, and I own this hotel. I noticed that hurricanes have been getting stronger and more violent, so I built this hotel to survive a severe storm. My own family is tucked away in quarters that I designed just for them. There are twenty-two of us here, including my great-grandparents."

"Thanks for taking us in. I hope our hotel room isn't too high up," said Matt. "My wife is afraid of elevators."

"Well, that won't be a problem," said Mr. Gardner with a smile. "The hotel rooms are all taken. All employees and their families were welcomed right after my family. Then the local people were taken in. I have turned the rest of the hotel into a rescue center for people who didn't have family up north that could take them in and six families of tourists, including you folks. There are eight hundred fifty people here besides the guests without rooms."

"If we don't have a room, where will we sleep?" asked Matt.

"Follow me," said William Gardner. He led them to a large banquet hall, being used as a dormitory. It was filled with long rows of beds.

"Why did they let us come?" Matt asked. "Why didn't they say anything at the airport up north?"

"They probably figured you had your reasons," answered Mr. Gardner. He led them down one of the long rows. "Here are your beds, numbers 21-26 in aisle 5. The seventh bed is right there, number 23 in aisle 6, head to head with this bed. Please keep your luggage on your own bed or at the foot of it. As you can see, everyone was issued one case of water. Be careful, because it has to last until the storm is over and we get the all-clear to leave."

"Can we buy any food?" asked Larry.

"There is no charge for you folks who don't have rooms. Follow me. I'll show you where to get food," said Mr. Gardner. He showed them windows that will open to serve food. "Food will be served at 7:00, 12:00, and 6:00 pm. You are to go in a single line and pick up your tray, using your own water bottle for a drink. Then take your meals to your bed to eat or to the conference center."

On the way to the conference center, the family was shown the bathrooms. There were no showers, but they were welcome to wash up in the sink. Mr. Gardner stopped by a small gift shop and grabbed a snack for each of them to eat, since they missed lunch. Then they went into the conference center.

The conference center was a huge room with stadium seating, a stage, and a large screen that stretched the entire width of the stage and rose to the ceiling of the room. "What you see on the screen is the live view of our south parking lot. The storm is getting quite nasty," said Mr. Gardner. "I hope you have a good stay. You should be quite safe in here."

The family went into the conference center and sat down to eat their snacks. Matt noticed that Rosemary was very quiet and wide-eyed. He remembered how nervous she gets around crowds. The scene on the screen was getting worse by the minute. Water was rising in the parking lot and the cars seemed to be sliding in one direction. Large pieces of debris were crashing into the cars and then flying off with the wind. Even in the middle of the conference center, which was on the first floor of the hotel, the non-ending roar of the storm could be heard, and it was upsetting many people.

The coverage switched from the parking lot to a news station. It showed the radar of the hurricane. The most upsetting thing was that the storm had barely moved into their area. The newscaster reported that the storm surge alone had changed the entire west coast of Florida, including the removal of houses and buildings of all kinds. And there was no longer electrical power or phone service west of Orlando.

Some people in the room were getting hysterical. Matt thought it might be better to keep people "in the dark" about what was happening outside. Then the news station switched to another part of the country. In the state of Washington, Mount St. Helens was erupting. A massive cloud of poisonous gasses was spreading and heading toward several large cities, and lava was pouring out of the top of the volcano as if the earth was emptying its contents.

Ken started yelling something at the top of his voice, but no one could understand him because of the roar of the storm. He pointed toward the door to the hallway and they all followed him out. "What's happening?" said Ken. "First there were the disappearances and now these unheard of natural disasters! Is God angry?"

"I don't know about that," said Matt. "But I have a very bad feeling that we could lose our power and be completely in the dark for days. If that happens, people will just go crazy."

"You know I'll go crazy," said Rosemary.

"We need to be prepared in case that happens," said Matt.

"I was just thinking the same thing," said Ken.

Just then Mr. Gardner came walking along,

obviously on some important mission. Matt got his attention and pulled him off to the side. "Mr. Gardner, I want you to know how much we appreciate you taking me in. But we might have a problem."

"What's wrong?" asked Mr. Gardner.

"Well my wife has a severe phobia of being in a crowd," said Matt. "I was wondering if you have any place in this hotel where the seven of us could be alone. Some of us could sleep on the floor and we could all squeeze in."

"As a matter of fact," said Mr. Gardner, "I do have one room available. One of my employees took his family and went north to be with their family instead of coming here." Mr. Gardner suggested that the young people sleep in the original beds out with the other people.

"I really appreciate this," said Matt. "But I think we will all stay together. How long could it last anyway? I mean, hurricanes usually go through in about a day, don't they?"

"Normally they last a day or two, but this isn't a normal storm, and these aren't normal times," said Mr. Gardner. "This one could last four or five days, or it could turn north and go up through the states." He pulled out a little notebook and told Matt that he will send seven meals to Room 156, where they will be staying. "Now go to the banquet hall and get your luggage and your water."

As they walked to the banquet hall, Matt told the family the discussion he had with Mr. Gardner and the good news that they had a room. When Josh heard the plan, he suggested that he and Larry and Rachel stay out with the rest of the people so they won't be so crowded.

"Think about it Josh," said Matt. "If the power goes out, you will be in darkness with a mob of frightened people. No, we are staying together. If we have to sleep on the floor, it will be worth it."

The family went into the banquet hall, and they tried to look inconspicuous as they gathered up their stuff and grabbed their cases of water bottles. Luckily, the few people who looked at them didn't ask where they were going. It was awkward carrying the water, but they didn't dare leave it behind. Finally they reached the room, and it was locked. Matt told everyone to sit down in the hallway outside of the room, and he would go in search of the key.

While Matt was gone, Rosemary started crying. Then she started sobbing. Josh and Lori remembered seeing her like this before. They moved to each side of her and tried to comfort her.

"Mom, listen, it's not so bad," said Lori. "We're better off than all those people because we are going to get a room."

"I have a confession to make," said Rachel.

Everyone looked at her wondering what it could be. She already told them how bad she was. "I know we aren't at Disney World," she began, "and I know things might get worse, but I'm having a really good time with all of you."

"Don't you get it?" asked Rosemary. "We're all going to die. Did you see the size of the hurricane? Did you see that volcano? God is mad at us, and he took all of those people, including Sydney, to some safe place before he lets us have it."

"Maybe God is trying to wake us up," said Lori. "Maybe he wants us to turn to him for help. If we were going to die, we would be out there in the storm. Mr. Gardner didn't have to take us in, and he didn't have to give us a room, with our own bathroom and with meals served to us. I think God is protecting us."

Matt came around the corner and held up a key to the room. Everyone got up and went inside. The room was very nice with two queen size beds, a sofa, and a chair. It even had a refrigerator and a coffee maker. Ken turned on the TV. The newscaster was telling about an earthquake in California that was worse than any in recorded history.

"I'm not even surprised," said Ken. "This is the worst hurricane in recorded history and that volcano in Washington is probably the worst one in recorded history. What else is going on in the world?"

"Turn off the TV a minute Ken," said Matt. "I need to talk to you all about something. If the power goes out, we need to stay right here in the room. Whatever you do, do not leave this room."

"Does anyone have a flashlight," asked Josh. "Just in case."

"Yes," said Lori. "I have a tiny flashlight on a little keychain."

"Good," said Matt. "Can you put it in your pocket so you can find it fast?"

"Got it," said Lori.

"Now I know we wouldn't be in this fix if we would have watched the news," said Matt. "We would be sitting and relaxing at Jack and Melinda's. But I still think it is a bad idea to watch the TV. It is nothing but bad news, and that just upsets us. What we need is some good news."

The family settled into the room. Matt and Rosemary took one bed and Lori and Ken took the other. In the TV side of the room, Rachel took the couch and Larry sat down in the chair. Josh was on the floor.

"You said that we need some good news," said

Rachel. "Would you like me to read my mom's Bible?"

Everyone was quiet for a while. Finally Matt said, "Rachel, I think that is exactly the good news we need."

Rachel opened her Bible to a section in I Thessalonians that her mom had highlighted and had drawn arrows pointing to it. "This is chapter 4, verse 16," Rachel said. "For the Lord himself will come down from heaven, with a loud command, with the voice of the archangel and with the trumpet call of God, and the dead in Christ will rise first. After that, we who are still alive and are left will be caught up together with them in the clouds to meet the Lord in the air. And so we will be with the Lord forever. Therefore encourage each other with these words."

"You know what I think?" asked Lori. "I think we missed the boat."

"What are you talking about?" asked Rosemary.

"Jesus came and took his believers," said Lori. "Sydney was a believer, and she was taken."

"Grandma and Grandpa too," said Josh.

Ken looked at Rosemary who looked like she was about to freak out. "Uh, Rachel, why don't you read something a little more encouraging?" suggested Ken. "Try something from the Old Testament."

Rachel stuck her fingers deeper into the Bible and opened it up. "Daniel," she said. "Oh good. Maybe we will read about the lions." She began to read right where she opened the pages, Daniel, chapter 12. "At that time Michael, the great prince who protects your people, will arise. There will be a time of distress such as has not happened from the beginning of nations until then."

"That's about all the encouragement I can take. Please don't read anymore," said Rosemary.

Just then someone knocked on the door. Everyone looked at each other in alarm. Matt walked to the door and called out, "Who's there?"

"I have your seven dinners," someone answered. "Do you want them?"

Matt opened the door, and the man wheeled in a cart with the meals. Everyone sat down to a delicious dinner of roast beef, mashed potatoes and gravy, carrots, rolls, and pudding for dessert. He even brought in iced tea and coffee for them to drink. The whole time they ate, they were silent, obviously upset about the storms and the Bible verses warning about a time of distress that would be worse than all others. What if this was that time?

Matt noticed that Rosemary barely ate anything. "Honey," he said, "the food is very good. Can't you eat more than that?"

Rosemary just shrugged her shoulders. She put her tray back on the cart and went over to her bed. She opened the covers and crawled in with her clothes still on. She was immediately asleep. The family turned off the light above her and moved into the part of the room with the TV and sofa.

"I'm glad she's asleep," said Matt. "It's always better when she sleeps than when she freaks out."

"While she's asleep, do you think we could watch a little TV? I just want to know about the storm," said Lori.

Matt turned on the TV against his better judgement. The storm had barely moved at all, which they all thought was bad news. After reporting on the hurricane, the news station reported on other natural disasters, not only the earthquake and volcano, but also a form of the plague that was spreading across Asia. The world population seemed to be decreasing rapidly.

CHAPTER EIGHT

Rachel continued reading her mother's Bible while she ate her dinner. Matt turned off the TV and said that since Rosemary is asleep, they can try reading the Bible again.

"Isn't it funny," said Ken. "Normally we would want to watch some exciting adventure movie or play video games or hang out at the bar. With everything that's happening, I just want to learn more about God and what's going on in the world."

"Oh, do you want me to read out loud again?" asked Rachel. "I was thinking about starting at the beginning."

Larry, Ken, and Josh all said they would really like that, so she started reading Genesis 1:1, "In the beginning God created the heavens and the earth." She read all about the creation of the world and Adam and Eve, until the point where they were kicked out of the Garden of Eden.

Just then the building was hit by a particularly strong gust of wind. It seemed like the entire hotel was shaking and the power went out. Instantly, some small lights came on in the room.

"Mr. Gardner thought of everything, I guess," said

Ken. "I wonder if he provided emergency lighting in the conference center and the banquet hall. I really hope so, because it would be frightening to be in the dark in a crowd." The building continued to shake, and even though the sounds of the storm were somewhat muffled, they could still hear them. Then they heard screaming and running.

"Don't open the door, whatever you do," said Matt.

The family was very thankful that Rosemary was still asleep. They continued reading in Genesis. They read about Cain killing Abel all the way through Noah building the ark. Then they read Genesis 7:1. "Then the Lord said to Noah, 'Go into the ark, you and your whole family, because I have found you righteous in this generation.'"

Suddenly Rachel stopped reading and said, "I knew it! We missed the boat just like Lori said. Jesus came and took all of those people to heaven and we are left here to face a flood of catastrophes."

Not one of them said a word but just sat there thinking. They sat there for a long time and then they drifted into a restless sleep. The storm was roaring outside and people were panicking in the hallways. The family dreamed of wind and rushing waters and all kinds of trouble. A loud sound combined with the shaking of the building woke them up. They were all holding onto pillows and cushions and each other, and a feeling of intense helplessness seemed to have gripped them all.

"I had a terrible nightmare," said Lori. "You weren't in it Ken. I was at a conference of some kind. Your sister was there, and I didn't even know she was coming. She had her three kids with her. Somehow, she broke into a hotel room, and asked me to come in and help her. She filled the tub, and put all three kids in the water, all the while I was begging her to get out of that room. Her baby tipped over and I rushed over and sat him up. Just then the director of our conference came in the door, with hotel security. They told us to get out of the private room and took me down to a basement area. Somehow, your sister and kids all slipped away. The director said that because of what I did, everyone in our group lost our rooms and our meals, and had to remain downstairs whenever we weren't in class. I felt so guilty! I knew everyone in my group was suffering because of my mistake. It was all on me."

"Can you even imagine how Jesus felt, just before he died on the cross?" said Ken. "He didn't sin at all, and yet he took on the sins of everyone, horrible sins."

"I read about that," said Rachel. "It's in Luke, toward the end of the book." Rachel took a few minutes to look it up and then read starting with Luke 22:41. "He withdrew about a stone's throw beyond them, and prayed. 'Father, if you are willing, take this cup from me; yet not my will, but yours be done.' An angel from heaven appeared to him and strengthened him. And being in anguish, he prayed more earnestly, and his sweat was like drops of blood falling to the ground."

"He did that for us, and it was so difficult that he sweat drops of blood," said Matt.

"Oh Dad," said Lori. "Why didn't we know this before? We would be with him now."

"We were too busy, I guess," said Matt. "Wasting a lot of precious time doing nothing good."

Lori looked at Rachel and asked, "Can't you find something comforting to read to us? Mom isn't the only one freaking out here!"

"Oh, I was just reading something interesting," said

Rachel. Then she read from Ephesians 5:8 and 9. "For you were once darkness, but now you are light in the Lord. Live as children of light (for the fruit of the light consists in all goodness, righteousness, and truth) and find out what pleases the Lord."

"I want to find out what pleases the Lord," said Larry.

"Me too," said Josh.

"But do you guys think we still have a chance?" asked Ken.

Josh said, "Maybe we could look up hope and see if we have any. Do they have an index in your Bible?"

Rachel looked in the back of the Bible and found a bunch of verses about hope. She turned to the fifteenth chapter of Romans and read verse 13. "May the God of hope fill you with all joy and peace as you trust in him, so that you may overflow with hope by the power of the Holy Spirit."

"Now I want to learn more about the power of the Holy Spirit," said Ken. "And I want to know if we can still get the Holy Spirit, to live in us."

Matt and Rachel were quiet for a while, looking through the index and checking out lots of verses. Finally Rachel said, "This comes from verses 13 and 14 in the first chapter of Ephesians. 'When you believed, you were marked in him with a seal, the promised Holy Spirit, who is a deposit guaranteeing our inheritance until the redemption of those who are God's possession- to the praise of his glory.'"

"I found one too," said Matt. "This comes from the end of the book of Matthew, and it's in red, so these are the words of Jesus. Verses 18 and 19 say, 'All authority in heaven and on earth has been given to me. Therefore, go and make disciples of all nations, baptizing them in the name of the Father and of the Son and of the Holy Spirit, and teaching them to obey everything I have commanded you. And surely I am with you always, to the very end of the age.'"

"There is something that bothers me in both of those verses," said Lori. "In the Ephesian verses, it says 'until the redemption of those who are God's possession.' And in the Matthew verses, it says 'to the very end of the age.' Maybe we are too late."

"He is with us always, 'to the very end of the age.' Maybe it isn't the end of the age. Even if we missed the boat, maybe it's not too late for us," said Rachel.

Suddenly there was a loud banging on their door. Larry got up to go see what they wanted, but Ken jumped up and grabbed his arm and put his finger to his lips. The family didn't move or make any noise as the banging continued. The men outside the door were cussing and pounding on the door and shouting for them to open up. It sounded like they were doing the same thing to the other doors down the hallway. The men said they would be back with something to tear the doors down.

After the men were gone, at least they hoped they were gone, Lori asked, "Why are they trying to get in here? What do we have that they want?"

"It's probably like road rage," said Ken. "Maybe they are angry that they didn't get their own room. But they should be so grateful that they aren't out there in the storm."

"Well, maybe the roar of the storm, plus the power outage, just got on their nerves," said Lori. "Look how

Mom is dealing with it." They were all amazed that Rosemary was still sleeping after all the pounding and noise.

"What can we do if they come back?" asked Rachel.

"They probably won't come back," said Matt. "They might go pound on some doors on a higher floor. Or maybe they won't be able to find anything to use to hit the doors."

Just then they heard the men in the hallway again. They started hitting a door down the hall with something very hard, which was making a loud crashing sound. The whole family was terrified and sat in their seats barely moving. The pounding got even louder and more rhythmic, like they were going to bombard the door until it gave way. Just when they thought they couldn't get any more scared, they heard a tapping sound on the door between rooms. They heard someone calling to them and knocking.

"What do you think that's about?" asked Josh.

Matt walked to the door, and asked, "What do you want?"

"Please let us come in," they yelled. "We need help."

Matt opened the door to see a terrified man and woman. "Please let us in," said the man. "Our door might not take much more."

Matt welcomed them and they closed both doors between the rooms and locked up. Ken noticed that the furniture wasn't attached to the walls, and he suggested that they get the dresser against the door. The men all moved the heavy dresser against the door and then they noticed there was another dresser in the part of the room where Rosemary was sleeping. They all pitched in and moved it against the door that goes to the hallway.

"Whew," said Josh. "No one is getting in either of those doors. Those dressers weigh a ton!"

The pounding sounded even louder and more rhythmic. "They are bound to get in because they are so determined and full of rage," said the man who had joined them.

"Do you know what set them off?" asked Ken.

"My brother is William Gardner," said their visitor. "He called and said there are about four inches of water in the banquet hall and the emergency lights are not very bright. The people are afraid they are going to drown in the dark."

"The pounding stopped," said Ken. "Do you think they got in?"

"I'm Brent Gardner, and this is my wife Jennifer, by the way," he said. "I don't hear anything next door, and I don't think they would be quiet in there. Maybe something drove them away."

"Please can we just stay in here with you?" asked Jennifer Gardner. "That door has to be badly damaged, whether they got in or not."

"Of course you can stay," said Matt. "Your brother has done so much for us."

Matt introduced everyone and then nodded toward Rosemary and told them that she had been sleeping for hours.

"I don't know how she can sleep, with all of that pounding, and the relentless sound of the storm," said Jennifer. "I can't get any rest. I'm a nervous wreck."

"Well," said Matt. "It's kind of an escape mechanism she does when things don't go her way."

"You folks were so quiet," said Brent, "that we weren't sure there was anyone in here."

"We've been reading the Bible since we got in here," said Matt. "We lost family members in the disappearances, so we are hoping to get some answers about what happened."

"We lost our three little boys when they were killed because their school bus driver disappeared," said Brent. "Jennifer hasn't been able to sleep at all since then."

"Well we never found their bodies," said Jennifer. "We looked in all the hospitals and then we went to the morgues. There were plenty of other kids there, but not our three. We just have to accept that they are gone."

"Maybe they disappeared," suggested Larry. "My Sydney disappeared."

"Well, the only children we know who disappeared went with their parents," said Brent.

"Who else do you know who disappeared?" asked Lori.

"My mom and dad disappeared right in front of my sister," said Jennifer. "The boys were so close to them."

"Maybe they are with your mom and dad," suggested Rachel.

"No. I think they got thrown from the bus and they are dead," said Brent. "We just didn't find them yet. I would rather believe that than think they are in a void some place."

"All I know is that I don't feel like living without them," said Jennifer. She started sobbing.

"Were your parents Christians Jennifer?" asked Rachel."

"Yes," said Jennifer. "Their faith meant everything

to them. I went off to college and I never went back to their kind of lifestyle."

"Well, I think your little boys are safe and sound in heaven with their grandparents," said Rachel.

"What makes you think they are in heaven?" asked Jennifer.

"Rachel, do you remember that scripture about Jesus coming and meeting people in the air?" asked Lori.

Rachel looked through her Bible and quickly came across the verse she was searching for and read it to Jennifer. "This is I Thessalonians 4:16. 'For the Lord himself will come down from heaven, with a loud command, with the voice of the archangel and with the trumpet call of God, and the dead in Christ will rise first. After that, we who are still alive and are left will be caught up together with them in the clouds to meet the Lord in the air. And so we will be with the Lord forever. Therefore encourage one another with these words.'"

Jennifer yawned and said, "Maybe they are safe with Mom and Dad and Jesus. I like that idea." She closed her eyes and went sound asleep.

Brent was so surprised. "Look at that," he said. "After being awake for four days, she falls asleep with all of us around her!"

"How about if we all get some sleep?" said Matt. "Brent, you and Jennifer can have the couch. Right kids?"

Josh, Larry, and Rachel all said yes. Matt gave out blankets and pillows from the closet. Rachel and Josh laid on the floor and visited quietly for two hours, sharing about Josh's broken relationships and Rachel's lack of relationships. Soon everyone was asleep even though the storm continued to roar and shake the building.

CHAPTER NINE

Saturday, Day Five

Around 9:00 am the next morning, they all woke to the sound of a cell phone ringing. They looked around the room, and finally Rosemary found the phone in her purse. "Hello," she answered. Rosemary listened carefully and finally said, "I don't believe it." She handed the phone to Matt, looking quite annoyed.

Matt took the phone and said, "Hello. This is Matt. Who am I speaking to?"

"This is Brook back in the neighborhood. Your wife gave me this number in case I needed to get in touch with you, and it turns out that I do. Jack and Melinda's son, Jesse, is alive! He's been in the hospital since Thursday. He was discovered in a state park with a badly sprained ankle and a concussion. He was pretty dehydrated and hungry. I guess he was on a field trip with his class at school and they thought he disappeared, when, instead, he slipped and fell off a rock. I just went over to check out their house this morning, and I saw the answering machine blinking. It was the hospital, trying to get in touch with Jack and Melinda. I don't want to be the one to tell Jesse that his whole family is gone, and I thought it would be better coming from you."

"Wait a minute," said Matt. "This can't be true. We were there. We saw his backpack and jacket on the floor and the mail scattered. He did disappear."

"I've been thinking about that," said Brook. "Something I remembered was the girl down the street. Jesse has been hanging out with her for years. She was always at their house. I don't know why I didn't think of her before. She must be the one who got the mail and then disappeared."

Matt was silent so long that Brook thought she lost him. She said, "Hello. Are you still there?"

"Yes," said Matt. She asked if he wanted the phone number of Jesse's hospital room. "Hold on. I need to find something to write on."

Matt was fumbling around. It was obvious to the whole family that he was upset and they were getting scared. Finally he found some paper, wrote something down, and almost said good-bye. But Brook stopped him.

"Wait," said Brook. "There is a problem not too far from here."

Matt rolled his eyes and looked around at the curious family. "What is it," he asked. "What else could be wrong?"

"Well, there is this sludge stuff pouring out of the ground up here in northern Ohio. It's kind of like quicksand. No one seems to know what it is. I didn't worry about it at first, but they talk about it on the news every night. So I thought you would want to know," said Brook, "so you can hurry up and get Jesse."

Matt thanked Brook and hung up. He looked at the family and at the Gardners, and awkwardly explained the phone call from Brook.

"This is going to ruin everything," said Rosemary. "Why didn't he vanish along with his family?"

"Mom, we have to go get him. We're all he's got," said Lori. "Dad, do you want me to call Jesse and tell him what happened to Jack and Melinda and his whole family?"

"I guess you'd better," said Matt, "but don't tell him that we moved into his house, used all their stuff, and even planned to take their cars. For now, just tell him that we are stuck in Florida and can't come and get him for who knows how long." Matt was embarrassed that the Gardners heard all that and looked over at Brent.

"Don't worry about us," said Brent Gardner. "None of us know how to act since the disappearances." The Gardners got brave enough to peek out in the hall and discovered that their door survived the pounding. They said their thanks and went back to their room through the hallway, using their key.

The family took turns in the shower and the men put the furniture back where it belonged. Lori was very eager to call Jesse, but Matt made her wait.

"I was thinking that maybe we shouldn't go back there at all," said Matt. "Can you think of anything of value that we left at Jack and Melinda's house?"

"Well our car is up there at the airport," said Ken.

"I'm going to call Jesse now," said Lori.

"No," said Rosemary. "Why does one kid need a big house and a store and at least four cars? Why didn't he just disappear like the rest of them?"

The family began arguing. Some thought they should just rent a car and start driving north, but others saw on TV that the storm now covered Louisiana,

Mississippi, Alabama, and Georgia. They sure didn't want to deal with the winds and rain anymore.

"This is my vacation!" shouted Rosemary. "We need to check out Disney World and if it's destroyed, we can go somewhere and sit on a beach. And when our vacation is over, we can move into Jack and Melinda's house, and Jesse will have to deal with it."

The family just sat there and stared at her.

"Mom," said Lori, "how can you think about vacation when Jesse is alive, injured, alone, and maybe even in danger if there is some kind of sludge going his way?"

There was a knock on the door and it was the guy delivering breakfast. "I'm sorry this is so late," he said. "We had a lot of trouble in the kitchen."

"Mom," asked Lori. "Can I borrow Aunt Melinda's phone? I need to call Ken's mom and see how they are doing. I promised I would call." Rosemary shrugged and looked at the phone on the nightstand.

Lori grabbed the phone and a muffin and headed for the door. Matt grabbed a muffin too and joined her going out the door. Larry, Josh, and Ken all smiled and dug into the big breakfast. Josh looked at Rachel and gave her a plate, while Rosemary went back to bed and pouted.

Out in the hallway, Lori took the phone and put numbers into it. "What are you doing?" Matt asked.

"I'm calling Ken's mom first," said Lori. "I told Mom I would and I don't want to be a liar." Lori mostly listened as Ken's mom told her how crowded they were with both girls and their families living there. She said good-bye without telling her that they were in Florida, something she wasn't very proud of at the moment.

"You really took the phone to call Jesse, right Lori," asked Matt.

"Of course," said Lori, as she began the call. Someone answered the phone right away. "Hi. Is this Jesse?"

"Yes. Who's this?" asked Jesse.

"This is your cousin Lori. You remember me, don't you?" she asked.

"Where are my mom and dad? Why haven't they answered the phone for two days? They never go away," Jesse asked.

"Jesse, what do you know about what's going on in the world?" asked Lori.

"Nothing. Not one thing. I've been lying in a state park. Why, has something bad happened to my family?" asked Jesse.

"Jesse, didn't you think it was a little strange that your school bus and all of your classmates and teachers left you at that park, and didn't have people out searching for you?" asked Lori.

"I haven't thought about anything else for days now," said Jesse. "Why didn't Mom and Dad come looking for me? And Beth? And Jamie? I can't believe they didn't turn the park upside down looking for me."

Lori could tell that Jesse was very upset. "Didn't the doctors and nurses tell you anything?" asked Lori. "Haven't you been watching TV?"

"No." said Jesse. "Tell me what's going on."

Lori didn't know where to start. "Jesse. People all over the world disappeared on Tuesday while you were at the park, so they probably figured that you disappeared too. I mean we thought that."

"Did mom and dad disappear?" asked Jesse.

"Yes," said Lori. "People were with them at their work and saw them disappear. They were there and then they weren't."

"What about Beth?" asked Jesse.

"We went to your house," said Lori. She saw her father give her an annoyed look, but she kept talking. "We went there to find out what happened to all of you because no one answered the phone. Did your girlfriend come to your house after school?"

"She came over almost every day after school," said Jesse.

"We came to your house on Wednesday. It was obvious that someone came in your house and dropped a huge backpack and a denim jacket on the floor by the door. The mail was scattered on the floor, and there was a bag of popped popcorn in the microwave. We thought that you did all of that and then disappeared." Lori thought she could hear Jesse sniffing. "Does that sound like her?"

"That was her," said Jesse. "Do you know that Beth and I have been together since fifth grade? So you think they all are gone? Mom, Dad, Beth, my brothers and sisters? What about Grandma and Grandpa?"

"Yes, all of them," said Lori. "Josh was with Grandma and Grandpa when they disappeared."

"Why are they all gone, and I'm still here?" asked Jesse.

"For the same reason we are all here," said Lori. "We weren't exactly Christians. We think Jesus came and took them all heaven. It was prophesied in the Bible that all the Christians on earth were going to heaven, and this happened all over the world."

"I was always going to do it. Once at church camp, I came really close to accepting Christ as my savior and getting baptized," said Jesse. "I don't know why I didn't do it."

"Well if you would have done it, you would be with your family right now," said Lori.

"I wish I would have," said Jesse. "I really wish I would have."

"Well, Jesse, when can you get out of the hospital?" asked Lori.

"Anytime that someone can come in a car and get me," said Jesse. "Can you come and get me?"

"No, sorry," said Lori. "We are actually in Florida right now. Why don't I call your neighbor Brook? I bet she will come and get you and take you to your home."

"That sounds good," said Jesse. "But I'm not sure I'm healthy enough to go home and take care of myself."

"We are trying to get home, but there is a huge storm between you and us. Expect a lot of rain this week, by the way," said Lori.

"How do I get in touch with you guys?" asked Jesse.

"This is your mom's phone that I'm calling on," said Lori. "Do you know her number?"

"Of course I know her number. What did you guys do?" asked Jesse. "Did you just go into our house and take whatever you wanted?"

"Pretty much," said Lori. "That's exactly what we did. We didn't know any of you were still around."

Jesse was silent. *He must think we are all lowlifes,* thought Lori.

"Well, are you going home to your house or my house?" asked Jesse.

"Our car is at the Akron/Canton Airport," said Lori. "So we need to go there first.

Did you hear about any slime or sludge coming out of the ground near where you live?"

"I thought I was hearing things," said Jesse. "I think I heard the nurses talking."

"Well if it heads toward you, go the other direction," said Lori. "Do you drive Jesse?"

"Yes I drive," said Jesse. "Maybe Brook can come and get me and drop me off at my car, which should still be at the high school."

"I'll call Brook now," said Lori.

"I can call Brook," said Jesse. "She is my neighbor."

"OK," said Lori. "I'll let you go now. But keep in touch until we come see you soon." Jesse said good-bye and hung up.

Matt and Lori finally stepped outside the hotel and they couldn't believe their eyes. There was debris everywhere they looked.

"How are we ever going to get out of here?" asked Matt. "I wish we never would have gotten the crazy idea to come down here."

"Dad, did you say it was only about ten miles from here to the airport?" asked Lori. "We could walk that far couldn't we? I walk three miles at the park with my friend sometimes. If we get up early in the morning, we could take our time and get there by evening. What do you think?"

"Your mother wasn't much of a walker when she was your age. I don't think she would do that now, to save her own life, let alone for a nephew who shouldn't even be alive, according to her," said Matt.

"Maybe it's time we split up," said Lori. "Some of us

can go back and be there for Jesse. Those who don't feel like a ten-mile hike can stay here until they clean up the roads and then just take a shuttle to the airport."

Matt knew she was right, but he hated splitting up. He knew he would be stuck in the hotel with Rosemary, and he would rather go to the airport and get back home.

When they walked into the room, the family was sitting there eating, just like when they left. "Lunch is here!" said Larry. They sat down and ate a nice lunch with the family. Finally it was time to tell them about the phone calls.

"I called your family Ken," said Lori. "Your mom said they are a little crowded but they are dealing with it." Then she told all about the conversation with Jesse. Everyone was quiet and thoughtful except for Rosemary. Finally she told them all what she thought.

"Why did he have to survive the disappearances and all the accidents?" Rosemary asked. "He's going to ruin everything."

"Mom," said Josh. "We all have each other. Jesse doesn't have anyone."

"He's right," said Lori. "He even lost his girlfriend. He's been with her since fifth grade. He's devastated."

"I say we take a shuttle to the airport right now, hop a plane, and go get him," said Josh.

"That sounds good to me," said Ken.

"Hold on a minute," said Matt. "You guys haven't been outside yet. The water has gone down, but the roads are full of cars, trucks, buildings, debris, and all kinds of things. I even saw a boat. If we go to the airport, it will be on foot."

"Well, we better get moving," said Josh. "It's a good

thing we packed light."

"I'm not going anywhere," said Rosemary. "I came here for a vacation and I'm not leaving until I at least get to sit by a pool or a beach."

"I'm going home," said Josh.

"Me too," said Lori.

"I go where Lori goes," said Ken.

"I guess I'm going too," said Larry. "We're all going together, aren't we?"

Matt was silent. He knew how it would go. *Couldn't Rosemary give in just this once? Of course a ten mile hike with her would be no picnic.*

"I have an idea," said Rachel. "I can stay here with Rosemary. You have all been so kind to me, and it's something that I can do for you. We can go to a pool or the beach. We'll figure it out. And we still have our plane tickets home, don't we?"

Matt looked at Rosemary and asked, "What do you think of that idea?"

"I think Rachel and I could have a good time," Rosemary said. "Go back to Ohio and rescue our poor little rich nephew. We'll come home eventually."

"It's only about 1:00 pm," said Ken. "If we leave now, we can get to the airport before dark."

"I'll call the airport and see if I can get our tickets changed for tonight," said Lori.

While Lori took care of the reservations, the rest of them packed up their things. In about ten minutes, they were ready to go. They remembered to take at least two water bottles each and a few snacks. Matt remembered to take Melinda's Bible. Lori was able to change the five reservations to a 7:30 pm flight from Orlando to Akron

Canton. She packed her bag and said she was keeping Melinda's phone, since Rosemary forgot to bring the charger for it, and she can pick up one at the airport.

Lori gave all of the important numbers to Rachel and she wrote down the hotel room number for herself to keep. They all hugged each other good-bye, and Rosemary didn't even seem sad that they were leaving her behind. Rachel looked a little sad but she said that she was happy to do something nice for the family. It felt good.

CHAPTER TEN

The family purchased a local map in the lobby before they left. It was warm and sunny outside as the group made their way across the hotel parking lot. Even though they had to jump over all kinds of debris and work their way around immense unrecognizable structures, they found themselves on Interstate 4 in a matter of minutes. There seemed to be less debris, so the group took off at a brisk walk. The first hour went by easily, and they were all laughing and singing as if they didn't have a care in the world.

Matt looked at his watch at 2:45 pm, and he was marveling that they could walk down a Florida highway and barely see any other people. Up ahead to the left, they could see a lake that was obviously over its boundaries. The water was flowing across the highway, but it was impossible to tell just how deep it was. Ken removed his shoes, tied the strings together, and threw them over his shoulder. He stepped gingerly into the water and was surprised that it had a fairly strong current. The water went up to his ankles, then to his knees. Then he banged into something, scraping up his right shin. He felt the object with his hand, but he couldn't tell what it was.

"You guys need to remember where this thing is, because it hurts like crazy when you run into it," Ken said. He continued on and finally he called back that the water was getting shallower. Matt and Lori began removing their shoes, but Josh and Larry looked kind of annoyed.

"What's wrong?" asked Matt.

"I don't want to get my jeans wet," said Josh. "It's my only pair."

"Well you have your backpack," said Lori. "Change into shorts."

"Right here in front of everyone?" Josh asked.

"Yes, and hurry up," said Lori. "This water has slowed us down."

Larry removed his shoes and socks, but decided to just go in with his jeans on. Soon they were all knee deep in water, walking to the right of Ken's path with hopes of avoiding the unidentified object that messed him up. They could see that Ken was on dry land now, and was putting his shoes and socks back on. Matt grabbed Lori's arm and shouted, "Hold on!" He pointed to their left and up ahead, and an alligator was gliding across the water toward Ken. They all started shouting for him to run. He took off running with one of his shoes still in his hand, running for his dear life. There was an abandoned car up ahead and he was determined to make it in one piece. The gator turned suddenly, and headed for the four of them.

The group turned around and began running back where they came from. They didn't see any big cars to climb onto in their direction, so their best defense was to put distance between themselves and the alligator. "Look for anything on the road that we can use as a weapon," shouted Josh. They reached the edge of the water and stepped onto the road, which was covered with sand, tiny rocks, and other debris. They looked back and didn't see the alligator.

"Where did it go?" they shouted to Ken.

Ken was standing on the hood of the car, looking in their direction, but he was too far away now to hear them. "What do we do now?" asked Lori.

They looked and looked, but they couldn't see an alligator anywhere.

"We didn't imagine it, did we?" asked Matt.

"No," answered Larry. "That was an alligator all right. He's out there somewhere, and we should see his eyes above the surface.

They stood there a long time, scanning the water. They were getting restless and had a sense of time being wasted.

"Should we try again?" asked Josh. "One thing is for sure. We don't want to be out here tonight."

"Yes. I think we need to try again," said Matt. "We need to find something to hit it with, if it comes near us."

There was plenty of debris around, so they grabbed pieces that were sharp or heavy, and stepped back into the water. It was getting pretty awkward for most of them, because they had gym bags instead of backpacks, shoes with socks stuck in them on their shoulders, various other things like maps and purses and water bottles, and now heavy or sharp objects for hitting alligators. The men all looked excited, like this was a great adventure, but Lori was terrified. She was frightened of most dogs, so this was like her worst nightmare. Her feet were cut and bruised, and she was shaking uncontrollably. Tears were rolling down her cheeks.

They got about halfway across when they spotted the gator, and this time it wasn't alone. Two big alligators were to the left of them, about the same distance as they were from the dry road ahead. They figured that alligators could swim much faster than the four of them could splash through the water. Lori froze, staring at the alligators and ready to take off in the other direction. Matt noticed her and he grabbed her arm. "Come on. It's now or never, and we aren't getting stuck out here at night," he said. When she resisted, Matt called for help. "Josh, come on. Let's get her out of here."

Josh dropped his club and grabbed her other arm, and they took off, dragging her through the water.

"Larry, we're not looking back, so if the gators get close, it's up to you to hit them," said Matt.

Larry was carrying a four-foot piece of tailpipe, but he wasn't stopping to wait for the alligators to catch up. He was taking long, high steps, and he noticed the water was getting shallower. "We're almost there," he shouted. He ran on ahead, out of the water, and dropped his load on the dry road. Then he turned with the tail pipe, ready to fight off the gators. Ken had jumped off the car and was there beside him, with what looked like a piece of metal shelving.

The alligators were closing in on the threesome, so Larry went back in the water on one side of them, and Ken on the other. They jabbed the gators with their weapons, hitting them in the eyes and on the head. Matt and Josh ran with Lori all the way to the car and put her up on the hood. She turned and climbed up on the roof.

"Stick that tailpipe in his mouth," shouted Ken, "and then run for the car."

Larry did that, but he found another club-like objet

on the road, and he went back to help Ken. While the one alligator struggled to get the pipe out of its mouth, the boys managed to hit the other one hard enough to get it to turn around. They took the opportunity to run. Larry scooped up his belongings, and soon they were all up on the hood of an old Dodge.

"Let's go before they start coming this way," said Matt.

"Don't bother putting your shoes back on," said Ken. "Look ahead."

There, ahead, was another Lake that had spilled over onto the highway. Everyone looked disappointed, but Matt looked at the map and said that this should be the last time they have to deal with water on the road. They just needed to get through this little stretch.

This time the water was so high that they couldn't tell where the highway went. Larry noticed that there was a green highway sign way ahead, so they decided to head straight for that. The water was knee deep and cold, but there didn't seem to be much of a current, and so far, there were no alligators. They walked this way for a good half hour, and just as they came out of the water, they reached an entrance to a highway going east. They looked at it for a long time and decided that they should walk one more mile to the Beeline Expressway, which went east to the airport.

It seemed like a good time to take a break. Matt looked at his watch, and it was 5:05 pm. This was going to have to be a short break. Lori gave everyone a muffin and a cookie, leftovers from the hotel meals. They drank their water, put on their shoes, and started their mile hike to the next highway.

"Remember when you guys were dragging me

through the water back there?" asked Lori.

"Uh, yes," said Josh. "You were scared out of your mind."

"I was," Lori said, "but did you notice that I ran out of the water? At first, you guys were dragging me and I was so scared that I couldn't move. I just started praying and asking God to help me. And then you know what happened? I just knew that God was with us, and we were going to be all right. My legs started working again, and I ran out of the water to the car. Then I sat up there praying for Ken and Larry, and soon they were running to the car too."

"Hey, do you guys notice anything about the road?" asked Josh.

"Yes," said Matt. "The road is clear. I think we are out of the storm area." They hiked in silence the rest of the way and came to the highway entrance that led east to the airport. Up ahead, they could see cars moving.

"If someone will just give us a ride, we can check in and have time for some dinner," said Ken.

When they reached the freeway entrance that went straight to the airport, the group decided that they won't ride with just anyone. They needed a van or minivan that could fit them all in.

"Here comes a van," said Larry. Everyone waved their arms and the driver pulled over and rolled down the window. There in front of them was the grizzliest character they had ever seen. He had long, dirty blond hair and a matching beard and mustache. There was something wild about the look in his eyes and the grin on his face.

"Where you folks heading?" asked the driver.

"Well, we were hoping to get to the airport,"

answered Matt. He was not sure he should have told the guy.

"I'm not going far, but I'll be glad to take you people to the next exit," the driver said.

"That's OK," said Matt. "I think we can find someone going all the way to the airport." The man gave them some kind of sign and sped away. Another car pulled up, and a nice-looking young man asked if they needed help.

"We need a ride to the airport," Ken said.

"That's where I'm going," he answered.

Everyone looked in his car. It looked like there was room for three adults, not five.

"You're welcome to squeeze in," said the man.

"We really are desperate," said Matt. "We have reservations on a 7:30 flight."

The man popped the trunk and they put everything in. Then Ken and Lori jammed into the front bucket seat, and Matt, Josh, and Larry piled in the back. They had to sit at an angle, because their three bottoms just didn't fit. Matt thanked the man and introduced the family as he drove away.

The man's name was James Rhodes. He told them that he lost his whole family five days ago. He said that his wife and twin girls meant everything to him, and he would give anything to get them back.

"I lost my daughter Sydney too," said Matt. "Larry here was her husband."

"Really," said James. "I'm going to Chicago to meet a man who claims to know where all our loved ones are. He said that he thinks he can get my family back for me."

Lori looked at the man and he looked educated. She

wondered how any intelligent person could fall for such a scam. She looked at Ken, and he gave her a subtle shake of his head, indicating that she shouldn't say anything.

"Where did you hear about this man?" asked Larry.

"On the internet of course," said James.

"What makes you think he's on the level?" asked Larry.

"He showed me a picture of a room full of people, mostly women and children," said James. "It looked real enough to me. Here we go to the drop-off area. Be ready to hop out and get your stuff. Maybe we will see each other inside."

"Oh, I sure hope we see you in there," said Matt. "Thank you so much for the ride. You saved the day!"

CHAPTER ELEVEN

The family went to check in and discovered that their flight was cancelled.

Matt approached a man who was handling luggage. "Excuse me sir," Matt said. "Can you tell me why they cancelled the flight to Akron/Canton?"

"There's some kind of junk, like lava, heading for the airport," he answered.

A lady at the counter overheard and told Matt that the people in a line across the room were booking on a replacement flight to Columbus, Ohio. She pointed to the line and said that it departs at 8:30 pm.

"Shall we just go to Columbus since our flight is cancelled?" Matt asked the family. "There's the line over there."

"If it's the best we can do," said Lori. "But then we will have to drive up to Jesse's."

"Some of us might just as well go home, since we will be so close," said Matt.

"No way," said Josh. "Remember Mom and Rachel will be going back to Canton. And don't forget about Jesse, who is all alone in the world."

"Well, I hope that stuff stops moving soon," said

Matt, "because Jack and Melinda's house and store are only a few miles south of the airport."

While the family was standing there in line, Melinda's cell phone rang. It was Jesse saying that Brook came to the hospital and got him and dropped him off at his little Mustang, which luckily was still at the high school. He was home now. Lori explained that they were at the airport, that the flight to Akron/Canton was canceled, and that they were in line to book a flight to Columbus. She also told him that they were planning to come and be with him, one way or another.

Ken grabbed the phone and said, "Hey, Jesse. What do you know about that slime junk?"

"The last thing I heard was that they think the stuff is coming from the bottom of Lake Erie," said Jesse. "They don't know why it is flowing, but they think it is slowing down. If the stuff gets any closer, Brook is going to her grandparents' farm, an hour south of here. She offered to take me along and I said if that happens, I will be glad to go with her."

Lori took the phone back and told Jesse to let them know if he has to leave town, but that they hope to see him soon.

The family booked the Columbus flight, went through security, and headed for the nearest fast-food airport restaurant. Larry spied James Rhodes, the man who gave them a ride to the airport, and took off after him. James was pleased to join their family. Soon, everyone was sitting around a large table, enjoying their meal. This was their first chance to relax since last night when they sat around the hotel room reading the Bible. It seemed like a long time ago.

"So James, did you check in for your trip to Chicago?" asked Ken.

"Yes, but I'm having some doubts," said James. "I don't know what's holding me back."

"James, was your wife a Christian?" asked Lori.

He looked startled at the question. "What difference does that make now?" James asked.

"Have you heard the theory that Jesus came and took all of his believers to heaven, and they are with him now?" asked Lori. "We think that the children of the ones who disappeared went with their parents."

James just sat there. The family ate their food and gave him time to digest the idea. Finally he said, "The truth is that we fought a lot. She wanted to go to church all the time and I didn't want her to go at all. When the girls came along, she insisted on taking them every Sunday. I felt angry and left out. But this idea that they all went to heaven is pretty hard to believe."

"So it's easier to believe that someone is holding all of the missing people of the whole world captive, and for a large amount of money, you can get your family back?" asked Ken.

"It's better than thinking that they are gone for good and that I'll never see them again," said James.

"We all missed the chance to go to heaven, but we are hoping that we will get a second chance," said Matt.

"Well, I have the money to get my family back, and I'm going for it," said James.

"I hope it works out for you," said Ken. "But if it doesn't, start reading the Bible and you'll find the answers you're searching for."

The family shook hands with James Rhodes, and

then headed for the area to wait for their plane. Lori stopped at a kiosk and bought a charger for her phone. Then she sat and charged the phone.

As the family waited, Lori looked at Josh and asked, "Are you OK, Josh? You haven't said much all day, and you seem kind of thoughtful."

"I'm all right," said Josh, "but I wish we wouldn't have left Mom and Rachel behind. We can't even call and find out how they are because your phone isn't charged yet."

Lori reached in her purse and pulled out the paper with the phone number of their hotel room. She gave it to Josh and handed him the phone attached to the charger. "Call them," said Lori. "See how they are doing."

Lori walked over and stood by Ken. "I wonder if he's really worried about Mom, or if all of this sulking is more about Rachel," said Lori.

Josh talked a few minutes, hung up, and sat down in Lori's seat by the charging station. The curious family moved closer to him to hear news about their mom and Rachel. "Rachel said that Mom wanted to take a nap, so Rachel fell asleep too. When she woke up, Mom was gone," said Josh. "She couldn't find a note or anything and she didn't know what to do?"

"What did you tell her?" asked Matt.

"I told her to check the gift shop or the bar," said Josh.

"That's really good advice," said Matt. "Your mother isn't what I'd call independent, so she should be back soon. She probably just needed a drink."

"Dad, I was just thinking that maybe I should just stay here in Florida, and go back to the hotel and help

Rachel take care of Mom," said Josh. "You know how Mom gets sometimes."

"No!" shouted Lori. "I know what you're thinking. You're thinking that Rachel is pretty cute and she really needs your help. Well, if you want to have a relationship with her, you need to go home, take care of Grandma and Grandpa's house, and get another job."

That wasn't exactly what Josh wanted to hear, but he sat there and didn't say another word about it. Soon their flight was called, and they all boarded the plane for Columbus, Ohio.

CHAPTER TWELVE

Rachel paced the hotel room, thinking that she really didn't want to go out looking for Rosemary. If Rosemary just went out shopping for something, she should be returning soon. Or she might be sitting in a bar for hours. *If I go out looking for her, I could miss her, and then she will wonder where I am,* thought Rachel. She sat down and turned on the TV.

Instead of the news, there was a comedy, featuring a bunch of friends hanging out together. This was Saturday night. A week ago, Rachel was hanging out with her friends, just like on the TV show. It seemed like years ago. Would it ever be like that again- carefree? Maybe people were already getting back to life as usual. Rachel realized that it would be easy to slip back into the old routine, and forget all about the Bible and Jesus and a life that means something. Remembering her mom's prayer journal, Rachel promised herself that she will read the Bible and pray and find her way to heaven, and nothing is going to distract her from that goal. She decided that it was time to go out and look for Rosemary.

The first place Rachel went was the lobby. She couldn't believe the change. People were checking in and checking out. The place wasn't boarded up anymore. She glanced out at the road and cars were moving. A quick walk around the gift shop let her know that Rosemary was not there. She asked for directions to the bar and was soon walking down a long corridor. Rachel was only twenty years old, so she peeked in the door, hoping no one would notice her. Immediately she spotted Rosemary sitting alone in a booth across the room. Two men at a table near Rosemary were having a loud argument. Rachel caught Rosemary's eye and motioned for her to come out. Rosemary held up her drink, indicating that she wasn't finished yet. Rachel moved away from the doorway and put her back against the wall. *I can't believe I volunteered for this,* she thought. *How did Josh and Lori turn out so normal?*

Rosemary finished her drink and decided that it was time to get back with Rachel and plan their vacation. Matt didn't leave her any cash, so she placed Melinda's credit card on the bill and waited as a young man took it and said he would be right back. When the waiter returned, he asked to see her ID. Rosemary didn't want to show the ID with her name on it.

"What's the problem," Rosemary asked.

"Is your name Melinda Walker?" asked the waiter.

"Oh, she's my sister-in-law. She gave me her card so I can enjoy my vacation," said Rosemary.

"Actually, the card has been reported stolen," said the waiter. "If your sister-in-law was reported missing by her place of employment, her assets have been taken by the government. This all happened yesterday. Didn't you listen to the news?"

"No, I didn't," said Rosemary. "Do you think I can go to my room and borrow money from my friend?"

"Why don't you just charge it to your room?" the waiter asked.

"Well, uh, I don't remember the room number, but I'm sure I can find it if you just let me go," Rosemary said.

"Not a chance," said the waiter. "I'm going to have to call security."

The rowdy man at the next table told him to "Leave the little lady alone." He said he'd be glad to pay her bill and buy her another drink.

Rosemary had a bad feeling about sitting down with the two men who had been arguing for the last hour, but did she have a choice? It was obvious to her that both men had been drinking too much.

"That was very kind of you to offer to pay my bill, but I really need to be getting back to my family," said Rosemary. "I'm sure they're very worried about me, especially my husband." She stood up and started to leave, but the one man grabbed her arm.

"You think we're just going to let you go?" said the man who had offered to pay her bill. "We expect a little gratitude for what I did for you. You would be headed for jail right now if it wasn't for me." He gave Rosemary an ornery grin, and she had a feeling of dread sweep over her. She thought she was going to throw up or pass out. The man saw the fear on her face and he roared with laughter, squeezing her arm even harder.

"Let her go Roy," said his friend. "We don't need her." He stood up and Roy shoved him back in his seat. A regular brawl was breaking out, and Rosemary got hit on the lip in the scuffle before she fell on the floor, as waiters and bartenders tried to restrain them. Rosemary saw her chance and ran out the door.

Once in the hallway, Rosemary started vomiting. She wiped her mouth and looked both ways. She couldn't remember how she got there. She went down the long hallway to an area that looked vaguely familiar. She caught her reflection in a mirror and was horrified at her appearance. Her mouth was swollen and bleeding, her eye makeup was smeared, and her hair was a mess. She had barf on her clothes and shoes. *Would this nightmare ever end?* She was shivering all over and afraid she might throw up again.

"Rosemary! Are you all right?" asked Rachel. Rosemary practically fell into her arms, shaking violently. "Let's get you back to the room."

Rachel helped Rosemary get into a nightgown and gave her a drink of water. Then she took a warm washcloth and dabbed Rosemary's face, removing makeup, blood, tears, and vomit. Rosemary was still shaking uncontrollably, so Rachel got her a blanket and wrapped her up in it.

"Why did you leave without letting me know?" asked Rachel.

"I needed a drink," said Rosemary.

"Did it help?" asked Rachel.

"It did help," said Rosemary, "until Melinda's credit card didn't work. Why didn't Matt leave me some cash? And then this horrible man said he would pay my bill and buy me another drink. The waiter left. And then I tried to leave, and the man grabbed my arm and squeezed it so hard. And then these drunk guys just started fighting and punching. He even punched me in the mouth. It was awful!" Rosemary just started bawling.

"Are you hungry, Rosemary?" asked Rachel. "You

missed dinner."

"I just want to sleep," said Rosemary.

So Rachel helped her into bed. Rosemary was still crying and shaking badly. Rachel wanted a shower so badly, but didn't trust Rosemary until she was sound asleep. So she sat down with her mom's Bible. Rachel tried reading, but her thoughts kept going to her own mother. *My mother never drank and was always there for me. Why, oh why, did I get so rebellious?*

CHAPTER THIRTEEN

The hurricane was now listed as a tropical storm, but it extended from northern Florida to the Ohio River. The family went to their seats on the airliner, with Ken and Lori sitting together and Josh and Larry sitting together. Matt went to his seat and found that he was sitting next to a teenage girl, who was around fourteen years old. When he sat down, she frowned and turned toward the window.

"Hello there," Matt said. The girl just shrugged. "Are you going to Columbus?"

"Aren't we all?" the girl asked. Under her breath, she said, "Stupid."

Matt realized this was going to be a long flight sitting next to Attitude Annie. He looked around the plane and it seemed pretty full. Matt thought, *Maybe I can ask the stewardess to move me, of course, I could get someone worse."*

As if the little brat could read his mind, she said, "What's the matter? No other seats available?"

"Oh no," Matt said. "I was just checking to see if my family is all settled in."

"Whatever," said the girl.

"Why are you going to Columbus by yourself?" asked Matt. "Did you family disappear or something?"

"No they didn't disappear, like I could be so lucky," she answered. "My sister is moving in with her boyfriend, and I'm not staying here with my mom and her live-in. My grandparents in Mansfield are taking me in."

"That's good," said Matt. "You should be fine there."

"What do you know about it?" said the girl. "It's just better than staying here." The girl turned her back to Matt and looked out the window.

The plane took off and went higher and higher, probably going over the storm. Finally it leveled off and the passengers relaxed. Matt went to sleep, exhausted from the day's events, and stressed about tonight's uncertainty. He slept a long time and dreamed that Rosemary was lost and wandering around dark alleys in Orlando. Suddenly, in his dream, two pit bulls were bearing down on his wife, and he woke up with a start.

The girl next to him said, "Hey, what are you worried about? You were groaning and wrestling around."

"Oh, my wife wouldn't come with us," Matt said. "And I had things to do that couldn't wait."

"What would make you leave your wife in Florida?" asked the girl.

"Greed." said Matt.

"What do you mean," asked the girl.

"My sister's family disappeared, and we are going there to take a few cars and other valuables," said Matt.

"Oh, I know all about that," said the girl. "My mom's boyfriend filled up our garage with all kinds of things that belonged to our neighbors who disappeared. I would like to see them come back and beat him to a pulp."

This was the first time Matt saw the girl smile. "You

must really hate the man," Matt said.

"You have no idea," the girl said. "When he's drunk or drugged up, which is most of the time, he's just mean. I hate him."

"Why does your mom stay with him?" asked Matt.

"I guess because he pays the bills," said the girl.

Matt noticed that the flight was getting quite turbulent. He looked back at Lori and she was clinging to Ken, obviously concerned. He could see lightning outside and rain against the windows. The "Fasten seatbelt" sign came on. Matt looked at the girl next to him, and she was smiling.

"Aren't you scared?" asked Matt.

"Not at all," she said. "I'm not afraid to die. I look forward to it."

"I hope you don't get your wish," Matt said. He pulled Melinda's Bible out of his bag and flipped to the Psalms for comfort. The girl rolled her eyes and looked out the window. The plane was descending rapidly, and it was bouncing around. The twenty-third Psalm, especially the part about the green pastures and the quiet waters, was very comforting. Suddenly Matt was homesick for his safe little place in the country. Maybe he should just go there and stay and lead a simple life again.

Matt felt a hand on his shoulder and looked up to see Josh. "Dad, Larry is in the bathroom throwing up. I guess he's airsick, if there is such a thing. Do you think he'll be all right?"

"He needs to get back in his seatbelt," said Matt. "Tell him to ask the stewardess for a barf bag."

"Gross, Dad, I think I'll leave him in there. Maybe he's safer in the bathroom," Josh said. "Do you think we'll be safe enough, Dad?"

"I'm sure we'll be fine, but get in your seatbelt," Matt said. Josh noticed the girl next to Matt and he hesitated. "Go Josh." Grudgingly Josh went back to his seat.

"You don't want your son to meet me, do you?" asked the girl.

"My son is always looking, and you are what, fourteen?" said Matt. "By the way, I am Matt Moses. What's your name?"

"My name is Lauren, and I am fourteen," she said. "Good guess."

Just then the plane shook violently. Matt looked back and saw Josh struggling to get off the floor and into his seat. Lightening was flashing all around. The pilot came on the speaker. "Please do not be alarmed," he said. "It seems the storm has arrived in this area, but we will soon be setting down on the runway. Please stay in your seats and keep your seatbelts fastened securely."

Lori closed her eyes and snuggled closer to Ken. He moved his arm and put it around her to keep her safe and to comfort her. Earlier today she felt exactly like this when the alligators turned toward them. It was time to pray again, so she closed her eyes and talked to God. She remembered to pray for Jesse and her mom, and asked God to help them land safely.

Matt looked back and noticed that Larry was not in his seatbelt yet. The stewardess was in her own seatbelt, and the look on her face was one of sheer terror. He wondered what she knew that they didn't. The plane was certainly bouncing around a lot for approaching the runway. He looked down at Melinda's Bible and noticed that some verses were underlined. He read to himself, "Even though I walk through the valley of the shadow of death, I will fear no evil, for you are with me, your rod and staff, they comfort me." Psalm 23.

Matt wondered if Melinda ever went through dangerous or depressing times. He kind of regretted the distance between them all these years. He wondered where she was, and if she was with Sydney and Mom and Dad. Matt thought about Rosemary, and he had a bad thought. He forgot to give her some money when he left, and he had all of the cash. Rachel had some cash, but would it be enough?

Suddenly the plane set down on the runway, and it was sliding and turning. The copilot came on the speaker and told them to assume the crash position by leaning forward and to cover their heads with their arms. Matt leaned forward and covered his head. He looked sideways expecting to see the girl's face, but it wasn't there. He looked up to see her defiantly sitting up. He reached up and pulled her down as he would with his own kids, and she didn't resist.

They slid off the runway, and the plane tipped up on its side. Matt was praying like crazy that the plane would not flip upside down. It was screeching and shaking, and the people were screaming. The seatbelts were digging into their bodies, as the plane strained to stop. Finally the plane came to a stop and slammed down on the ground with a loud bang.

Matt felt his body whip down and knock the air out of him. He struggled to sit up and get a breath. Finally he made a squeaking noise and the air got through. He realized that his neck really hurt. The girl next to him undid Matt's seatbelt and helped him down the aisle and onto the inflatable slide. It was pouring outside and very windy. They slid down the slide and Lauren led Matt toward an ambulance. He realized what was going on and stopped and turned to look for his family. Lori and Ken and Josh were right behind him.

"Dad, are you all right?" Lori asked, yelling to be heard above the roar of the storm.

"I think your dad hurt his neck," said Lauren.

"Thank you so much for looking after him," said Lori.

"I'm fine," said Matt, "but where is Larry?"

"I tried to go back and look for him," said Josh, "but the stewardess wouldn't let me through."

Everyone was drenched, but still they all watched as people slid down to the ground. Finally they saw a body lowered down the slide on a stretcher. Sure enough, it was Larry who was injured. The ambulance pulled up and they loaded him in, telling the family that he will be taken to St. Ann's Hospital in Westerville.

"Don't you think that you should go too?" shouted Lauren. "You should have your neck looked at." The rescue worker heard her and insisted that Matt get in the ambulance with Larry.

"We'll get a cab, Dad, and come to the hospital," said Josh. "See you there."

Inside the airport, Ken, Lori, and Josh signed a release form and headed out to catch a cab. Lori saw the girl who helped her dad walking with an older couple, and she was sorry she couldn't talk to her again.

At the ER Matt was examined and released. The doctor didn't think his neck was injured enough to warrant a brace, but he did give him a prescription for pain medicine. Larry's injuries looked worse than they actually were. The cuts on his face and arms, caused by crashing into the mirror in the bathroom, were cleaned up and bandaged, but none were serious enough to need stitches. He had bruises all over his body from being tossed around in the tiny space, but he also was released.

"How do you feel?" the family asked Larry.

"I hurt all over my body," said Larry, "but I guess I deserve it for not going to my seat. I was embarrassed because of a little barf on my clothes. I'm ready to go home, wherever that is."

"I can't call any of my uncles for a ride, since it's almost midnight," said Matt. "The question is, should we take a cab to my house or to Grandma and Grandpa's."

"Grandma and Grandpa had a dependable car, so let's go there," said Lori.

In the cab, the family talked about how God took such good care of them. The plane could have flipped over and caught fire, and they could have been killed. The usual key to Grandma and Grandpa's house was missing, but Josh had another way to get in, climbing up the pole to the upstairs deck and going in the sliding door. They pet the cats and found beds and soon they were all sound asleep.

CHAPTER FOURTEEN

Sunday, Day Six

Jesse woke up at 7:00 am on Sunday morning. The first thing he did was turn on the news to hear the latest on the northeast Ohio sludge. A high ridge runs through the north part of Ohio, so the sludge was moving southward. It had been approaching the Akron/Canton Airport, and people were moving out of the area. But for now, it stopped.

Jesse sighed with relief and jumped into the shower, because he had an overwhelming desire to go to church. Just a week ago, everything was fine. His family got up and went to church together like every Sunday. Jesse's Sunday School class was fun as usual. They teased the girls and tortured the teacher. He and his friends had been together since the baby nursery. Jesse wondered if any of them would show up today.

Twenty-five minutes later Jesse pulled into the church parking lot. The door was locked, but the custodian came and let him in.

"Why the locked doors?" Jesse asked.

"Some young punks have been coming in and

making messes, just for fun, I guess," said Danny, the custodian. "So I'm just keeping the doors locked."

Jesse looked into the sanctuary and it was completely empty. He asked Danny, "Are you and I the only ones left in this church?"

"So far, we're the only ones to show up," said Danny.

Jesse walked down the aisle of the sanctuary and went up on the stage. He sat down and began playing the hymn "It is well with my Soul." As he played, the tears rolled down his cheeks. He hadn't allowed himself to cry about his missing family, and now he wasn't able to stop. When Jesse ended the song, he noticed two of his church friends coming up on the stage. They were Andrew and Will. They sat down on stools that normally were occupied by the praise team. They both noticed Jesse's tears and they were very sober.

Will said, "That song has always been one of my favorites. Did you lose your whole family too?"

Jesse could barely answer. Finally he said, "Yes. It's like it just sunk in. They aren't coming back. I'm all alone."

"I don't have anyone left in my life," said Andrew. "This is the one place that we always came to together. I feel so alone in that big house. I miss my mom and dad. I miss my little brothers so much."

"Jesse, can you play another song?" asked Will.

The three guys sang hymns and praise songs for over an hour. The words never meant so much to them before. Heaven was calling them because that's where their loved ones were. It was time for the second service and a few other people came in. They came right up on the stage too and joined them. Jesse played a couple of the songs from the first service. Many people were crying. Will stood and asked if he could read some Bible verses that meant a lot to him.

He began reading Ephesians 1:3. "Praise be to the God and Father of our Lord Jesus Christ, who has blessed us in the heavenly realms with every spiritual blessing in Christ. For he chose us in him before the creation of the world to be holy and blameless in his sight."

Will paused a moment, looking over the scripture. A man who came in for second service asked, "Do you think it's too late for us?"

Finally Jesse said something. "I don't think it's too late. I was always going to accept Christ as my savior. I just never got around to it. Well, I don't want to put it off any longer. Is there anyone here who would be willing to listen to my confession and baptize me?"

Andrew spoke up immediately and said, "I'm ready too if God will take me."

"I'll baptize you guys if someone will baptize me," said Will. Everyone there, twelve in all, headed for the dressing room to slip into gowns.

Jesse was the first in line, and Will was there to baptize him. Jesse said, "I believe that Jesus is the Christ, the Son of the Living God, and I accept him as my Lord and Savior."

Will had heard that many times before, and knew his part well. "Upon your confession, I baptize you in the name of the Father, and of the Son, and of the Holy Spirit, for the forgiveness of sins, and the gift of the Holy Spirit." He lowered Jesse under the water and raised him back up. Jesse turned and did the same for Will after his confession. Andrew was next, and then another, and then another until all twelve were baptized. They all changed back into their clothes and met by the front door.

"I don't really want to go home alone," said Jesse. "If any of you would like to pick up your favorite fast food and come over to my house, you are very welcome." Many of them were interested, so Jesse gave them directions, picked up a cheeseburger and fries, and then rushed home to check on the condition of his house.

Most of the people ate and then went home, but Will and Andrew hung around longer. They talked a long time about the disappearances and the messages from God through hurricanes, earthquakes, volcanos, and even sludge. They talked about God's will for their lives now. They tossed around the idea of rooming together, and they agreed to keep their church alive. All three guys went to different schools, and none of them had returned to school yet.

Will and Andrew still had jobs, but Jesse worked at Chick-fil-A, which was a Christian fast food restaurant. Most of the people who worked there were missing, including all of the owners and managers, so the restaurant was closed. Jesse needed to find a new job, not only for the income, but also to keep from going crazy. A week ago, Jesse was trying to decide which college to attend, and now he wasn't sure college was important. Will and Andrew felt the same way. They decided to meet together every day to pray and study the Bible, until they figure out what God wants them to do with their lives. The guys went home and Jesse was left alone with many questions.

Something was bothering Jesse and it was his financial security. How was he going to take care of his big house and pay the bills? It bothered him that his aunt and uncle and cousins had helped themselves to things in the house and they were planning to come back again. He decided to do a little investigating. He went into the kitchen and turned on the TV. The sludge had stopped moving and geologists believed it was done. Jesse was relieved, because it seemed important for him to take care of his parents' property.

Jesse reached up into the cubbyholes over the desk and pulled down the bills. He laid them out on the counter top. Then he went out and got the mail and added a couple things to the pile. Everything was fairly simple. There was an electric bill, gas bill, water bill, and a sewer bill. There was a payment statement for Stephanie's college and one for Jamie's college. He could throw those away. There were church envelopes and quite a few envelopes for payments to missionaries. He might need the church envelopes if they get it going again, but the missionaries are probably all gone. He didn't see a house payment or any credit card bills, but he figured they would be coming.

Jesse ran upstairs to see if his dad's billfold was there. It wasn't there and he hoped it went with his dad when he disappeared. There was an envelope with the words "mission trip to Haiti." It was empty! Dad was planning to go on a mission trip next January, so there was probably a lot of money in there. Jesse had a pretty good idea who took that money. He found his mom's purse in the living room. He went through it and was frustrated that her credit cards were missing. He remembered that Aunt Rosemary took his mom's cell phone, so she probably took her cash and credit cards as well. Then Jesse found his mom's checkbook.

Suddenly Jesse had a thought. His mom and dad

probably had a will. He opened the file drawer and there it was in the very back. He studied it carefully and discovered that his parents left everything to him and his brothers and sisters, to divide evenly. This included the house, the store, and all of their possessions. Since he was left alone, everything was his. Once again the tears flowed down his cheeks. Jesse went over to get a tissue, and noticed that the answering machine was blinking. The first message was from Lori saying that they would be coming to help him soon. *Do they think I'm twelve years old?* The second message was from a pharmacist friend of his dad. He heard that his store was closed and figured out that he disappeared. He offered to buy the business and said that he had arrived at what he thought was a fair offer.

Jesse decided that it wasn't too late to call, so he picked up the phone and called the man about the store. It rang and then the man answered.

"Hi, this is Jesse Walker. Did you call me?" he asked.

"I sure did. I'm Terry Harold, a close friend of your dad's," he said. "I'm so sorry for your loss. Do you have any family members left?"

"No," said Jesse. "Just aunts and uncles and cousins and they don't live around here. I'm all alone."

"That's tough," said Mr. Harold. "I lost my parents and I miss them a lot. But I still have my wife and kids."

"Have you been to Dad's store?" asked Jesse.

"Yes, I went there and got the number of a customer who locked up the store after your dad disappeared," said Terry Harold. "I called the man named Earl Jones and he said that a man named Matt Moses came by and said he was your dad's closest living relative. He and his boys took the van and left."

"They would have taken the store too, if they could," said Jesse. "At least the van is sitting out front, but who knows where they left the keys."

"Well Earl has the keys to the store and he will give them to the new owner," said Terry Harold. "And I hope that will be me."

"If you want to buy the store, Mr. Harold, I will be happy to sell it to you," said Jesse.

"Please call me Terry," he said. "I already called my bank and I was approved for a loan for the business and for the building. I do have another idea though."

"What's your idea, Terry?" asked Jesse.

"I was thinking that I could buy the store and the building from you myself," said Terry. "I have the same accountant as your dad. We could hire a lawyer to draw up the agreement, and I could probably pay it all off in about seven years."

"That sounds good to me," said Jesse.

"It's a good deal for you," said Terry. "I will pay you the interest instead of the bank. I'm pretty sure your dad told me that your house is paid off, so you can easily live on what I pay you each month. I'll get back to you with the exact amount after I talk to the lawyer."

"Well you are doing me a huge favor," said Jesse. "I wouldn't have known where to look for someone to buy the store. Thank you so much."

"Jesse, I want you to know that I would rather have your dad back as my friend any day, than buy his store," said Terry Harold. They said their good-byes and once again Jesse could feel the tears falling down his cheeks. But Jesse did feel a huge weight lifted off him by selling the store and having an income. His parents taught him to be a good steward and to take care of his things.

Jesse went to the front of the house and looked out. He could see his Mustang, his dad's van, Jamie's Explorer, and Stephanie's car. He knew his mom's car was in the garage. He went to the file drawer and found a file named automobiles. He dug out all five titles. His car was the oldest and he would like to have something reliable that he could get around town in. Five cars for one. He should be able to pull that off and not have a car payment.

Suddenly, he had a troubling thought. Why was Stephanie's car here? Shouldn't it be in Kentucky? Is it possible that she is still here? Why did that thought bother him so much? He could use the company. Then Jesse realized that he felt a lot of comfort that his whole family was in heaven together and all he needed to worry about was getting there and taking a few people with him. No. If Stephanie was still on earth, she would be right here in the house. She's gone all right.

Jesse put the five titles in a bag, along with some checking account statements and paid credit card receipts that he found in the files. Now he can put everything in his own name, and not have to worry about greedy neighbors or relatives taking control of his life. He felt like a responsible adult. *Mom and Dad would be proud of me*, he thought. *But from now on, it's God I'm trying to please, and it was God who sent Jesus to die for me.*

CHAPTER FIFTEEN

Things were not going so well for Matt and the kids. They woke up Sunday morning and got ready to head for Jack and Melinda's house. They went down to the garage to get in the car, and it was not there. They all just stood there and stared at the empty garage. They opened the garage door, and it wasn't in the driveway either. They went back in the house and Matt tried to call the Snyder family, the neighbors who agreed to look after the cats. Unfortunately the phone was dead. Did someone cancel his parents' service? He walked right out the door and headed for the Snyder's house. Lori, Ken, Josh, and Larry all sat down on the sofa. They turned on the TV and flipped through the channels. What they saw was a variety of the most disgusting images they could imagine, mostly featuring sex and violence. They turned it off and went into the kitchen.

"I guess a nice McDonald's breakfast is out now," said Josh.

"It was a good plan, but I guess we won't be going through any drive-through restaurants, since we don't have a car," said Lori.

"You know, when I was here last, there was food in

the cupboards. It looks like someone has been helping themselves," said Josh. "Not only are the cupboards bare, but the refrigerator is pretty empty too."

"That takes a lot of nerve, just going into someone else's house, and taking their food and cars and who knows what else," said Larry. They all got quiet as they realized that was exactly what they did at Jack and Melinda's. They didn't feel too guilty though, since they didn't know that Jesse was still alive at the time.

Matt came in the house and slammed the door behind him. "No one answered the door at the Snyder's house." He said. "They are probably out joy-riding in Mom and Dad's car." The kids told him about the food shortage in the house and he got even angrier. "I saw a guy down the street and he said his phone is working. Why isn't this phone working?"

Larry looked at Matt. "My motorcycle is over at your house. We can use it to get around, one person at a time."

"Well, maybe we should go home. At least we have some food there, and the telephones should work," said Matt.

"It will take a good thirty-five minutes to walk it," said Josh. "I've made that walk often enough over the years."

"How about the rest of you?" asked Matt. "Do you want to check out your place or just come home with me?"

"I'm sticking with you," said Larry. "I told the landlord that Sydney disappeared and I'm not coming back. I got out everything I need, which isn't much."

"Josh, you could just stay here and look after the place and take care of the cats," said Matt.

"Maybe I will," said Josh.

"Ken, what do you think we should do?" asked Lori.

"Our car is at the Akron/Canton Airport," said Ken. "If you get your grandparents' car back, at least one of us should ride along and bring our car home. About where we're going to live and what we're going to do, I don't know. I feel kind of lost."

Even though they were ready to travel early Sunday morning, the family spent the entire day searching for a car to drive and food to eat. That night they went to sleep, bored and frustrated, with Ken and Lori at their place, Matt and Larry at Matt and Rosemary's house, and Josh at his grandparents' house. To make things worse, it started pouring again, with wind and lightning and thunder. The weatherman said that it might last two or three days. This was a nightmare.

CHAPTER SIXTEEN

Sunday was a beautiful day in Florida. Rachel asked Rosemary if she would like to try to find a church, and Rosemary admitted that she was never very comfortable in church. Rachel promised her that they could leave if she was uncomfortable, but Rosemary said that she wouldn't go.

"Well, what would you like to do?" asked Rachel.

"Do you think we could go to the beach?" asked Rosemary. "I long to go to the beach."

Rachel always hated the beach. She hated being hot, and she hated baking in the sun. She especially hated having sand all over her body. And more than anything else, she hated wearing a bathing suit in public. Rachel was born shy about her body. That was the main reason she was so comfortable wearing black leather. This was not going to be pleasant, but she promised the family that she would take care of Rosemary.

"I'll tell you what," said Rachel. "You get showered and dressed, and I'll go see if I can arrange for us to get to the beach."

Rachel walked up to the lobby and asked if there was a way for them to travel to the beach.

"Well, the west coast is a disaster, so I recommend that you rent a car and drive to Daytona Beach, and then come back to Orlando to fly out."

"Oh, that's a good idea, since our reservations are at the Orlando Airport. Thanks," said Rachel.

Rachel was already tired of entertaining Rosemary and being away from the rest of their family. The clerk at the desk helped her rent a car and reserve a motel room in Daytona for two nights, and change her flight reservation to Tuesday morning instead of next Sunday. When Rachel told Rosemary about the arrangements, she was disappointed that they were going home in two days, but she was excited about staying a block from the beach.

Rachel was a little concerned about money. She made sure they checked out of the hotel before 11:00 am and that they packed their own lunches using leftovers from the hotel meals. They grabbed as many water bottles as they could carry and walked to the lobby, where they picked up their car. Rachel wished that Rosemary would read the Bible aloud to her as she drove, but Rosemary turned her body toward her car door and immediately went to sleep. They arrived in Daytona and soon they were setting up a spot on the beach. Rosemary was so happy that it was almost worth all the trouble.

Rachel was dressed in shorts and a T-shirt. She was hot already and hoped that she would sleep a couple hours and wake up when it was time to leave. After a while, though, Rachel woke up, and she was roasting. She looked at Rosemary, who was smiling and very contented. Rachel got up and walked across the hot, burning sand to the water. She waded in and splashed water on her arms and legs and face. That didn't really cool her down much, so

Rachel waded in up to the bottom of her shorts. She reached down and cupped her hands to splash a lot of water on her face. What she got was a jellyfish that stung her chin and neck and hands. She screamed with pain and staggered out of the water.

A man standing nearby recognized the remnants of the jellyfish, and knew the danger she was in. "Let me see your neck, where you were stung," said the man. Rachel was in terrible pain and collapsed onto the sand. The pain shot through her whole body, but the pain was especially bad on her chin and neck.

Rachel looked over at Rosemary, who was sound asleep. "Please," Rachel whispered, "Wake up my friend over there."

The man ran over and woke up Rosemary, but came back immediately to stay with Rachel. Finally Rosemary came over and looked at Rachel. "What's wrong with her?" she asked.

"She was stung by a jellyfish," said the man. "We've called an ambulance because she was stung on her neck. If it starts swelling, she could suffocate."

"Oh no," said Rosemary. "I have to go with her. I don't even know how to get back to the hotel."

The tears were running down Rachel's cheeks as she struggled to deal with the pain. She looked at her hands, which were swelling up. "Is my face swelling up as much as my hands?" she asked.

"It is swelling," the man answered, "but you don't seem to have any breathing problems. We will see what the paramedics have to say. I'm sure they see this kind of thing all the time."

The lifeguard was notified of the problem and made

everyone get out of the water. He came up and examined Rachel and put a kind of paste on her wounds. The ambulance arrived and the paramedics came rushing across the beach. They looked at the injured areas and asked how long it had been since she was stung. The man guessed that it was about seven minutes ago. They said that Rachel was probably going to be fine, but that she needed to go home and sleep it off. They mentioned that she was very fortunate that she was stung on the side of the neck instead of the front.

"How long will the pain last?" asked Rachel.

"That's different for everyone," said the paramedics.

"I don't think I can walk back to the hotel," said Rachel. "I barely have the energy to stand up."

The paramedics recorded all of Rachel's information, and then they took her and Rosemary back to the hotel. They even took them to their room. They gave Rosemary some instructions about keeping the wounds dry until tomorrow. Even if she begged, Rachel had to wait until tomorrow to take a shower. "Oh, and give her lots of water to drink," they said.

After the paramedics left, Rosemary looked at the clock, and it was only 3:30 in the afternoon. Rachel was curled up on her bed, sound asleep. "What am I going to do the rest of the day?" Rosemary said out loud. She went to the phone and called home. She wasn't surprised that no one answered, because they were probably at Jack and Melinda's by now. She forgot to write down that number, so she called Matt's parents' house, just in case they were there. All she got was a busy signal. "What does that mean? I'm not going to spend the day watching her sleep," Rosemary said. She picked up her purse and walked out the door.

CHAPTER SEVENTEEN

Monday, Day Seven

Jesse showered, dressed, and finished with breakfast. He was just sitting in the kitchen, reading his Bible, and waiting for a call. Finally the phone rang and it was Terry Harold. They arranged to meet at his dad's store at 10:00 am. Earl James was going to be there, and the lawyer. Jesse grabbed the store folder and the bag that contained the five car titles and everything that he could find about his parents' checking accounts, savings account, investments, and the house deed, along with the will, proving he was the heir.

When Jesse arrived at the store, an older man got out of a car, and shook his hand. "Well you don't need to show me any identification," said Earl. "You look just like your dad. I'm really sorry for you, left all alone, without your family. At least I still have my wife, Wilma."

I would like to thank you, Mr. James, for looking after my dad's store," said Jesse. "If it weren't for you, I wouldn't even have a store to sell to my dad's friend. The money from this store will support me and my work with our church."

"You have a church?" asked Earl. "Wilma and I wanted to go to church yesterday, but we didn't know where to go."

Jesse told Mr. James all about his church and the twelve of them who were baptized yesterday. Jesse got his phone number and promised to call about a Bible study they will start this week.

Then Terry Harold pulled in, with his lawyer. Earl let everyone into the store and showed them how to turn off the alarm. Then he gave Jesse the keys and left.

"I'm ready to sign the papers, if you are," said Terry.

They signed all the necessary papers and shook hands. Jesse gave Terry the folder that contained all kinds of store information, from the computer company to the place where they purchase support socks. Jesse invited Terry and the lawyer to church next Sunday, and Terry said that he and his wife will be there.

Jesse mentioned that he was trying to get his finances in order. The lawyer advised him that he might need to apply to the state of Ohio to get money back from his parents' bank accounts, since the government was taking funds from all accounts of people reported missing by their workplace. He said to get his house and belongings in his own name. There were rumors that the government was also planning to take the property of people who disappeared.

Jesse thanked the lawyer for the good advice and shook hands with him and with Terry Harold. Then he got in his car and went to his favorite car dealer, who was a friend of the family. He sent four of his salespersons home with Jesse, and they returned with all five vehicles. The dealer looked them over carefully, and told Jesse that he could pick out any new car on the lot in a certain price range. Jesse went to that lot, and finally made a decision. He purchased a seven-passenger SUV with a DVD player. Jesse could picture himself driving all kinds of people to church events and youth activities.

It took visits to four different banks for Jesse to get his affairs in order, but he was successful. One bank did contact the state government and got Jesse's money back from his mom's account, since her school had reported her missing. Jesse looked at the activity on his dad's debit card, and figured out that it was the work of his aunt, uncle, and cousins. He was totally amazed that they could blow so much money in such a short period of time. The banker did some research and discovered that there were reservations for two for a trip from Orlando to Akron/Canton and that they were on his dad's account that they were closing. When Jesse heard that his Aunt Rosemary was on that flight, he decided to cancel that account after the ticket purchase was honored. The balance would then be put into his own checking account.

Jesse considered it a blessing that the government had taken control of his mom's account, because the relatives weren't able to use that money. Everything was now in his name and he could stop the insanity. He pulled out of that last bank in his new SUV, praying for God's wisdom in running his life.

Jesse pulled into his driveway and stopped to get the mail. There was a gasoline bill in the mail. He opened it and discovered that someone had charged gas on the bill since the disappearances, and he knew it wasn't him. Jesse went straight to the telephone and canceled all of the old gas cards, and set up one new account in his name. The new credit card would arrive in a few days.

Will called and said that he and Andrew were going to Wendy's for a quick dinner, and asked if Jesse wanted to join them. Andrew was leading the Bible study Wednesday, and they had four people their age joining them. Jesse felt kind of bad because he didn't invite anyone to Bible study. Of course, he did invite Earl and his wife and Terry Harold and his wife to church on Sunday.

All day long Jesse had an idea at the back of his mind. It was time he went back to school. That was the only way to meet people his age and bring them to the Lord. He decided to start tomorrow. The school administrators would feel pretty guilty about leaving him in the park on that field trip. They should have looked harder for him. He was lucky to be alive. Jesse jumped in the car and headed for Wendy's. It was pouring outside and he was a little early, but he enjoyed sitting there in the car reading his Bible.

In the parking lot, Jesse opened his Bible to the book of Acts and began reading verse 42 of the second chapter. "They devoted themselves to the apostles teaching and to fellowship, to the breaking of bread, and to prayer."

It is almost like Will and Andrew and me, Jesse thought. *We are devoting ourselves to the work of the Lord.* Jesse looked forward to spending the evening with his friends, studying God's Word, and then getting up in the morning and going back to school.

CHAPTER EIGHTEEN

Matt woke up on Monday morning and looked out the window. Almost a week ago, he stood in this same place, looking out at the calm countryside and refusing to believe that Sydney was gone. Instead of just six days ago, it seemed like weeks. Yesterday was frustrating, but today, he was almost glad to be back home. The rain continued to fall, and Matt had no desire to go out in it. The phone was working, but he couldn't call Josh, since that phone was dead. He had no idea how to get in touch with Rosemary, but he was glad that she was in Florida, probably enjoying the sunshine.

Matt reflected on the direction of his life. Since Jesse was still alive, the things that belonged to Jack and Melinda rightfully belong to Jesse. It was fun having a van for a while, but he can get another car. He enjoyed having travel money, and treating the family to a nice vacation, but it was just a dream. Matt didn't really want to take on raising Jesse, a teenager. After all, Matt thought, I already raised my kids. Another thing that Matt did not want to do was go back to that job. He hated that job, but he is going to need some kind of a job, and a reliable car. He pulled Jack's credit card out of his pocket. He looked at it, and walked over and cut it up.

Larry walked into the room. "How long do you think these rains will last?" he asked.

"After a hurricane, rain can last for days," Matt said. "I've been thinking that we should just forget about Jack and Melinda's place and all their stuff. Jesse is still alive, so it all belongs to him."

"That's all right," said Larry. "I don't mind staying here. It's just that every place I go reminds me of Sydney. I miss her so much. While we were traveling around, I just pretended we were apart."

The winds were really picking up and the lightening was flashing.

"Here we go again," said Matt.

"This time, no one is going to serve us three meals a day," said Larry. "I really enjoyed that family time in the hotel. I wasn't very worried about the hurricane."

Just then, someone was knocking rapidly on the door, and turning the handle. Matt ran to the door and opened it. Ken rushed in, thoroughly drenched.

"Lori's out in the car." Ken said. "Do you guys want to go with us? We're on our way to get our car from the Akron/Canton Airport. We'll probably try and stay with Jesse."

"Couldn't you give me a little warning?" Matt asked.

"We tried to call, but our phone service must have been cancelled like Grandma's," said Ken. "We don't know what's going on."

"We haven't even had lunch yet," said Matt. "I don't want to go out in this weather. Why don't you guys just come in and wait it out?"

"You know Lori when she gets an idea in her head,"

said Ken. "She borrowed my sister's car, and we're going. I think she's more worried about Jesse than she is about the car." Ken was shivering from the cold and rain.

"It's cold out," said Matt. "Didn't you bring a jacket?"

"I couldn't find it," said Ken. "We think someone's been going through our stuff too."

Suddenly, lightning blasted and hit something very close. A huge branch fell out of the tree and landed on the car that Lori was sitting in. It smashed the windshield, and covered most of the car. Ken, Matt, and Larry all ran outside to get her out. They couldn't even get close on the driver side, but on the passenger side, the door was blocked as well. The guys were all shouting and Lori didn't seem to be answering. Ken looked in the side window and saw that she was lying flat down on the seat and that the tree was on top of her. He couldn't tell if she was conscious or not. The branch was so massive that they couldn't budge it.

"Call 911," Ken shouted. Larry ran in the house and came back out immediately.

"The operator said no one is coming," said Larry. "All of the ambulance drivers in our area are missing. They are trying to hire others, but they haven' found anyone yet. She suggested we call a tree company."

"Then do it," shouted Matt. Larry turned to run back in the house, and his feet slipped in the mud. He landed on his bottom, and his hands sunk in the mud on each side of him. Lightning was still flashing all around them, and the wind and rain made it nearly impossible to function.

Ken remembered that he had the car keys, so he clicked the doors unlocked. He could open the back seat door about four inches. Looking in, he could see that the back seats fold down. He reached in and pulled down one of the back seats. Then he popped the trunk and climbed in. Ken worked his way through the car and got close to Lori. He thought he could hear her making sounds, but the storm was so loud he couldn't be sure. He reached the seat releases on both seats and pulled them back as far as they would go. It was a tight squeeze, but he was able to pull Lori onto her back and then out over the seat. Ken crawled backwards, pulling Lori through the car and then out of the trunk.

When Ken and Lori went in the house, Matt was yelling at a tree guy who refused to go out in the weather. Matt hung up and ran over to see Lori. She was drenched, filthy from tree debris, and bleeding from glass. And she was shaking all over.

"My body aches from being stuck in that uncomfortable position so long," said Lori. "I was cold and wet and now I can't feel my hands or my toes."

"Lori, I'm going to get you in a hot shower," said Ken, "as soon as we pull all of that glass out."

"I'll get your mom's robe and start the shower for you," said Matt.

They took turns showering, with Lori going first. They put on warm clothes and wrapped up in blankets. Lori had band aids on her arms and forehead, and she ached so much that she could hardly walk. They all had hot chocolate and soup for a late lunch, and then they fell asleep.

When Matt woke up, it was really dark out. He looked at his watch and it was 8:30 at night, with the storm still raging outside. Matt thought about Rosemary. It certainly seemed odd that she hadn't called him yet. He went to flip on a light, and there wasn't any power. He tried the phone, and of course it was out too. Matt felt a chill creep over him. No power, no light, no heat, no communication, and the rain continued to pour. How were they even going to get through this night? Matt decided to lie back down and try to sleep the night away, and maybe things would be better tomorrow.

Ken and Lori woke up in the middle of the night. They were sleeping on a futon in Lori's old room. Her mother had turned the room into a sitting room the minute she moved out. The futon wasn't very comfortable, especially for Lori, who was experiencing considerable back pain. They felt their way into the kitchen and found a candle and matches in a cupboard. Ken checked out Lori's injuries. The cuts were all fairly superficial, except for a deep one on the back of her head. Ken took a candle and found a couple of pain pills for Lori in the medicine cabinet.

"I don't know what I would do without you Lori," said Ken. "I was so worried. You know I love you."

"I love you too," said Lori. "What frightens me most about the close call is that I'm still not ready to die. That night in the hotel, when we were all reading the Bible, we should have accepted Christ."

"Those people next door joined us. Remember?" Ken mentioned.

"That's right," said Lori. "From what I've been reading, I don't think we have to stand up in a church to accept Jesus as our savior. You know, don't you Ken, that I believe that Jesus is God's real son, and that he died for everyone who believes?"

"I believe that too, Lori," said Ken.

"But, you know Ken, I want to go back to Jack and Melinda's house," said Lori. "I don't know why it seems like the right thing to do. I know we probably won't get a free car, and I know Jesse might not want us to move in and take care of him, but I feel drawn to the place anyway. Do you think there's still a way we can go now that Susan's car is wrecked?"

"As soon as it stops raining, we can get a tree company to come out and remove the tree," said Ken. "Then we'll get the car repaired. I hope Susan has insurance."

"Things aren't working out very well, are they?" said Lori. "Maybe we aren't supposed to go to Jesse's house."

"Listen, we have to get our car back, don't we?" said Ken. "Let's get some more sleep. Everything looks better in the daylight."

CHAPTER NINETEEN

Rachel woke up at 5:00 am on Monday morning. She got up, walked into the bathroom, and flipped on a light. Rachel almost fainted when she saw her face in the mirror, all red and swollen.

"Where am I and what happened to me?" Rachel asked herself. "I feel like I was hit by a truck."

Rachel came out of the bathroom and looked around the dark room. Everything came back to her: the trip to Daytona, the beach, and the jellyfish sting. Not only was Rosemary missing, but her bed looked like no one slept in it. "Not again!" Rachel said.

Rachel took a quick shower and got around. She grabbed the hotel key and ran out the door. Two guys in the elevator looked pretty scary, but they seemed more afraid of her. Rachel looked at the mirrored wall. Her hair stood out like a porcupine because she blew it dry so fast. Her face was swollen and she looked like she had no neck at all. In the lobby, people were coming and going as usual. Rachel didn't know where to start looking. The gift shop was still closed at this early hour. Didn't Rosemary learn anything from her last experience? Outside, there were sidewalks in both directions, leading to shops, restaurants, bars, hotels, and tourist traps of all kinds. Was this a place for a young girl, even a scary looking young girl, to be walking all alone? At 6:00 am, there seemed to be more people coming in from their night activities, than early risers beginning their day. Rosemary might be one of those coming in, so Rachel thought she should keep looking. But where? *This is just a waste of time*, thought Rachel. She went back to the hotel room, and threw the key on the bed.

One more day and I'll be back home, thought Rachel. She grabbed her mom's Bible out of her bag, and began looking through it.

Rachel began reading John 14:18. "I will not leave you as orphans; I will come to you." This was the first time Rachel realized that she's an orphan now. For a while, she felt like a part of Matt and Rosemary's family, but right at this moment, she felt like the orphan that she was. But the Bible says that he won't leave us as orphans. Next Rachel looked up her name in the concordance, and she turned to Genesis 29. She was fascinated as she read the story about Jacob falling in love with Rachel and working seven years for her hand in marriage, only to find that Rachel's sister Leah was given to him instead. Rachel was also given to him in marriage, and Jacob worked another seven years for her. She read on and on, finding that Jacob was an ancestor of all the Israelites, and it was through his offspring that Jesus Christ was born. She read so long that she found herself very hungry.

Rachel held a cool washcloth on her neck and was relieved that the swelling was going down a little. She took time and fixed her hair, so that people weren't afraid of her in the elevators. She grabbed her purse and the room key and headed out to find a fast food place to eat.

Walking along the sidewalk, Rachel stopped and peeked into a hotel lobby. Something told her to go in and look around, and there on one of the sofas was Rosemary. Rachel ran up to her and Rosemary looked very relieved.

"What are you doing here?" Rachel asked Rosemary.

"I couldn't remember which hotel we were in," Rosemary said. "They all look the same to me. I've just been sleeping here since last night."

"I can't believe no one bothered you," said Rachel. "They just let you sleep here in the lobby?"

"Well, I told them that this was my hotel, and I just couldn't remember your last name," Rachel said.

"Good thinking," said Rachel. "How about some lunch?"

"I'm starving," said Rosemary. "Where can we go? I saw a really nice place next door." Rosemary led Rachel to a fancy sit-down restaurant.

"I'm sorry, but I'm a little short on cash," said Rachel. "Do you have any?"

"Matt didn't give me any cash," said Rosemary. "He just went off and left me penniless.

But we have a few credit cards, don't we? Let's just charge it."

"Let's just eat a cheap meal at McDonalds," said Rachel. "We never know how long those credit cards will work. The account could run out of money, or we could reach their credit limit. Let's just use the cash while we have it and save the cards for emergencies."

They went into McDonalds. Rachel asked Rosemary what she wanted, and Rosemary pouted and said she would just have a side salad.

"I thought you were starving," said Rachel. "Don't you want a sandwich or nuggets?"

"I think I'll wait until I get home," said Rosemary. "Matt always takes me where I want to eat."

Rachel felt like she was dealing with a strong-willed child instead of an adult. She ordered the salad for Rosemary and a value meal for herself. She was so hungry that the food tasted really good.

It was 2:00 in the afternoon, and Rosemary wanted to go back to the beach. She said that she was in enough gift shops yesterday to last a lifetime. Rachel really did not want to go to the beach ever again, but she also knew that she had to stick with Rosemary from now on. They had to make that plane home tomorrow. After that she could hand her over to Matt to take care of. Rachel's own home was pretty inviting right now. *After this week I will be just fine living alone and taking care of myself,* thought Rachel.

They got through the afternoon. Rachel stayed away from the water this time and she got quite sunburned. Rosemary got a beautiful tan and thoroughly enjoyed the time at the beach. Rosemary even got in the water a couple times, but she didn't have any trouble at all. Rachel insisted that they go back to the hotel and get ready for bed early, because they had to drive back to the Orlando Airport in the morning. They picked up deli sandwiches on the way back to the hotel for tonight's meal and granola bars for breakfast.

Once again, Rachel put a sofa in front of the door to sleep on, so that Rosemary stayed put. Rosemary saw the arrangement and just laughed. Rachel decided to shower in the morning, because Rosemary should be sleeping soundly by then. Rosemary watched a couple movies, and Rachel tossed and turned. Her face and hands still hurt from the jellyfish stings,   and her sunburn burned like crazy, especially with the sand and salt still on her body. She longed to take a shower, but didn't trust Rosemary at all. Rachel finally fell asleep, but she had horrible nightmares that probably went along with Rosemary's movies.

Rachel was suddenly afraid of dying. She prayed to God, thanking him for sending Jesus to die for her. From now on, she planned to be God's girl. With such comforting thoughts she finally drifted off to sleep.

CHAPTER TWENTY

Tuesday, Day Eight

Jesse got up early on Tuesday morning and got ready for school. It was still pouring outside. *Would it ever stop raining?* One week ago he went on that field trip to the state park where his classmates and science teachers left him to rot in a deep crevice. Luckily a family was out looking for their missing dad and discovered Jesse instead.

Jesse went to the office first thing, and asked to see the principal. It was a large school, so Mr. Reynolds didn't recognize him. Jesse told him that he was Jesse Walker, and that he was left injured in a state park a week ago while on a school field trip, and that he was recently released from the hospital. The principal appeared shaken up, and Jesse figured that he was probably worried about a lawsuit.

"Please don't worry about it, Mr. Reynolds," Jesse said. "I just wanted you to know that I'm back in school today. We had good insurance, so most of my bills will be paid. Here is a copy of a hospital bill, and I was hoping you will accept it as an excuse for my absences. You see, my entire family disappeared. I'm the only one left, so I don't have a mom or dad to write an excuse for me.

"That will be just fine Jesse," said the principal. "How are you feeling now and how are you getting along on your own?"

"I had a concussion and I was dehydrated, and my ankle is still swollen, so I limp a little," said Jesse. "I sure do miss my family, but I'm taking care of things."

"That's good," said Mr. Reynolds.

"I do have one favor to ask, though," said Jesse. "I want to start a Bible study for students who have lost family members in the disappearances or for anyone interested. Could someone read this in the morning announcements?" Jesse handed him a card with the invitation on it.

Mr. Reynolds wasn't happy about the Bible study, but he was going to allow it, probably to keep Jesse happy and involved and not thinking about a lawsuit. Whatever the reason, Jesse was going to begin his Bible study today, right after school.

Jesse went straight to his homeroom, really sad that he could no longer hang out with Beth. If only he had given his life to Jesus sooner, he would be with her now. Many of the students were surprised to see him and came running up to him. He explained that he was injured and left in the state park for a couple of days, and then he recovered in a hospital, only to find out that his entire family disappeared. One of the guys apologized for leaving him there, but that they found out about the disappearances. It just made sense that Jesse was one of them.

They all sat down and listened to the morning announcements. The boy who read Jesse's card laughed and threw it down on the table, as if it was some kind of a joke. Jesse was really disappointed, but his Bible study became the topic of discussion all day long. The rumor around school was that Jesse lost his whole family and that he thought that he could join them soon by following Christ. One group of kids made fun of him, but there were quite a few students who told Jesse they will attend his Bible study.

There was another group at the school that was harder to deal with. They wore all black with leather jackets or hooded sweatshirts. They all dyed their hair black and wore it hanging in front of their eyes. There was a wildness about them that sent chills through Jesse. Word reached them about Jesse, and all day long when they saw him, they pushed him, punched him, or made threats to harm him.

The group was called the Pythons, and two of the students, a girl and a boy, used to be on Jesse's swim team. He wondered how they got involved with this group. And he wondered why the group was targeting him. The teachers didn't seem to know how to handle the group, but they almost seemed to like the group more than they liked him. Several teachers were hostile to Jesse and tried to humiliate him in class. *What is happening to this world?* Jesse wondered.

The school day finally ended, so Jesse headed to the library where he was to conduct the Bible study. About ten students came in and they were all strangers to Jesse. Everyone in the group lost at least one family member. They admitted right off that school had been torture since the disappearances and they were all considering dropping out.

"Why do they hate the Christians?" Jesse asked.

"I don't know, but today was the worst. Your announcement this morning seemed to bring out all kinds of animosity against us. And they seem to know we're Christians and they consider us their enemies," said one of the guys.

The group talked it over and decided that they needed to meet first thing every morning to pray that they make it through the day. Then they will meet every Wednesday night for Bible study at Jesse's church. They spent the next hour getting acquainted, exchanging phone numbers, and sharing their stories.

Jesse left school that day a little concerned about the danger of just going to school. Was it worth it? Was a high school diploma even important, considering the state of the world? That morning Jesse went to school excited and confident and now he was coming home confused, scared, and lonely. He was especially lonely and he missed his family and Beth. His mood was matched by the weather. It had been raining for days. He went into his house, curled up on the sofa, and went sound asleep.

CHAPTER TWENTY-ONE

Matt, Larry, Lori, and Ken woke up to the roar of the storm. They wondered if they were in danger of a tornado, because of the violence around them. Matt remembered a little, battery-powered radio that Josh had as a teenager, and went to search his old room by candle light. He found the radio and Lori borrowed the batteries out of both TV remotes to get it going. They tuned to a local station and learned that a tornado had struck a town just west of them and was headed in their direction.

"Rush to the basement everyone," shouted Lori. They hurried and were careful to keep their candle burning.

"Don't forget to close the door at the top of the stairs, Dad," said Ken.

"Got it," shouted Matt. "Anyone remember which corner of the basement we should go to?"

Suddenly a pole of some kind came crashing through a little basement window. It scared them all and came close to Larry. "The corner that has no windows, over there," said Larry.

"That's right," said Ken. "Let's all crawl under the table. It will give us more protection."

"Yuck," said Lori. "It's wet under here, and I bet there are all kinds of bugs too."

They could hear all kinds of crashing and banging above them. The storm was so loud that they could barely hear each other. The flames blew out on their candles, so they were in total darkness. The roaring continued and they wondered what they would find upstairs. Finally the sound changed from earth-shaking crashing to a constant vibration.

"What's that sound?" asked Matt.

"I'll go up and find out," said Larry. "It sounds like a hard rain."

"Be careful!" shouted Lori. "There are all kinds of things on the basement floor, like dumbbells and ping pong balls and now debris from the ceiling."

Larry carefully went across the floor and up the stairs. Matt re-lit the candles and Ken and Lori came out from under the table. Larry shouted for them to come up.

The family could not believe their eyes. Everything was gone, including the house, the garage, and the barn.

"Well there is good news, other than the fact that we survived a tornado," said Ken.

"What could that be?" asked Lori.

"We don't have to call a tree man anymore to remove a tree from Susan's car because the tree is gone, in fact all the trees are gone," said Ken.

"Her car is gone too," said Lori. "I wonder where it landed."

"We don't have to call a phone guy either," said Matt, "because the phones are all gone."

"I guess you and mom will want to live at Grandma and Grandpa's house now," said Lori, "unless you have homeowners' insurance. If you do you can build a new house right here."

"No homeowners' insurance," said Matt. "I don't know what we'll do."

"Bummer," said Larry.

Matt looked toward his neighbors' house and it was gone too. "We need to check on the Smiths," Matt said. "They didn't disappear, so they were probably home for the storm. Do you kids want to go back down in the basement to get out of the rain?"

"There is nothing here for us, Dad. We might as well come along and find a way back to our apartment," said Lori.

It was daylight now, so the four of them walked down the road to the Smith's place. They called down into the basement, but no one answered. Larry went down and looked around, but the neighbors weren't there.

Just then a car approached. It was Josh in their grandparents' car. He rolled down the window and asked, "Dad. What happened?"

"A tornado happened," said Matt.

"How did you guys survive?" asked Josh. "It looks like everything is gone."

"How about taking us to our apartment, and we'll tell you all about it on the way," suggested Lori.

The family was soaked, so Josh turned on the heater and headed for Ken and Lori's place. Matt told how they woke up in the dark and found their way to the basement just before the tornado struck.

"You guys were very lucky," said Josh.

"Luck had nothing to do with it," said Lori. "We all woke up at the same time. What are the chances of that happening? God spared our lives."

"I agree," said Ken. "I'm a night owl and never wake up early in the morning. Only God could do that."

"Mom is going to be really upset when she hears that the house is gone," said Lori. "Think about all her collections."

"Let's go get our car back and see if God has a purpose for us in Canton, Ohio," suggested Ken.

"Josh, will you drive us to the Akron/Canton Airport to get our car?" asked Lori. "Maybe Jesse will put us up for a night or two."

"I need to go too," said Matt. "In a few days your mother and Rachel will return to that airport. I should be nearby when they arrive."

"Can I go too?" asked Larry.

"We'll all go," Lori answered.

"Josh. How did you ever get Grandma and Grandpa's car back?" asked Matt.

"Oh, that was really fun," answered Josh. "One of the cats woke me up really early this morning to go out. When I let it out, I saw a set of keys by the back door and I figured they were to the car. I got to thinking about the Snyder family, and I remembered their jerk of a son named Bobby. Remember him? He was a couple years older than me and such a bully. Anyway, I looked him up in the phone book, and, sure enough, he lives on Johnson Street. I put the keys in my pocket and took a little walk. As I got near the house, I could see our car sitting out on the street. I just pushed the clicker, unlocked the door, got in, and drove away. It is our car, isn't it?"

"It is our car," said Matt. "Nice detective work, Son."

"I did one other thing, Dad. I changed the locks on Grandma and Grandpa's house," said Josh. "The Snyder family took our car and never even checked on the cats that we know of, so I don't trust them. I'll give you all a copy of the keys. I made extras."

"We may all end up staying there," said Matt. "Thanks for taking care of the place."

Josh drove Ken and Lori to their apartment, and Matt and Larry to the grandparents' house. Everyone got dry clothes on and packed to go to Jack and Melinda's place again. Josh put out lots of food and water for the cats and plenty of fresh kitty litter. He kept the car in the garage, just in case Bobby Snyder came by.

Finally, around two in the afternoon, Josh, Matt, and Larry arrived at Ken and Lori's apartment. The couple came out with large bags this time, as if planning to stay for a while.

"What's all this?" asked Matt.

"Ken and I both feel that God is calling us up north for something. We are prepared this time," said Lori. "Come on in and have a little lunch."

"We checked our checking and savings accounts and we are out of money," said Ken. "So we don't dare stop for food. We're going to try and find some work near Jack and Melinda's, and if we can't, we'll have to go back to our jobs at Walmart."

After they ate up all the food in the cupboards, they piled in the grandparents' car and left. Josh pulled into a gas station and looked at his dad.

"Oh, I guess that's my clue to pay at the pump," said Matt. He pulled out Melinda's gas card and swiped it. It was turned down. He pulled out one of his own credit cards, and it was turned down too. "I guess the party's over."

Matt went inside and paid cash for twenty-five dollars' worth of gasoline and they filled the tank and took off. Matt shared that he was now officially out of money. Josh said that he was down to his last six dollars and Larry said he had no idea if he had any money in the bank, but he had about four dollars in his pocket.

The family was silent on the two-hour trip to the airport. Most of them were homeless, jobless, and almost penniless. They weren't sure why they felt drawn to northeast Ohio, but most of them thought that God was leading them there.

As the family approached the airport, Josh shouted, "Everybody wake up!"

There, across the entire sky, was a beautiful double rainbow.

"I have a feeling that we are going where God is leading us," said Matt. The whole family felt the same way.

CHAPTER TWENTY-TWO

Rachel woke up Tuesday morning at 5:30 am. She was thankful that the alarm didn't go off yet, because she wanted to shower while Rosemary slept. In all of her life, Rachel had never enjoyed a shower so much. She was washing away sand, salt, dirt, and sweat. She was washing away the past two or three days of frustration and emptiness and a strange feeling of loneliness. Today she was going home. She was hoping that Rosemary's family would be there, so she could turn her over to them.

By 6:30, Rachel was clean, dressed, and packed. She looked in the mirror and was relieved that the swelling had gone down from the jellyfish sting. Her hair looked cute and her sunburn gave her a glow. She didn't know if she could allow herself to feel some hope.

It was very difficult to wake up Rosemary and inspire her to get cleaned up. Rachel finally told Rosemary that she was leaving for the Orlando Airport at 7:30 am, and if she wasn't ready to go, she would have to find her own way back to Ohio from Florida. Rosemary grudgingly got in the shower and was ready to go on time. They loaded their car and pulled into the nearest gas station. Rachel looked through the cash and cards in her purse. She decided to try her dad's gas card and was very relieved when it worked.

When Rachel got back in the car, she said to Rosemary, "I hope we don't get hungry before we get home. I just have a little cash left." She expected a response, but Rosemary was already sound asleep. Rachel drove toward the airport. She tried to find a Christian radio station, but everything she heard was full of swearing and profanity. She decided to try to remember some of the Bible verses she had been reading, but they just wouldn't come to her. *I am going to study a lot harder when I get home and start memorizing scripture,* she said to herself.

Rachel decided to pray silently for wisdom. "Dear Lord. I am beginning a new time in my life. Help me to be more responsible from now on, like an adult, and help me to know how much money I have and not spend what I do not have. Lead me to a group of believers. I really need a church group. Help me to find a job and a direction for my life. If you have any special work for me to do, for you Lord, please help me see it. In Jesus' holy name. Amen."

They went directly to the car rental station and returned the car. Then they took the shuttle to the airport check-in area with more than an hour to get through TSA and to the gate. Rachel held her breath the whole way through, so scared that something would go wrong and she would never get home. Soon they were sitting down, waiting for their plane.

"I'm so hungry," said Rosemary. "Don't you have any credit cards we can use?"

"I don't have any cards that I can use safely," said Rachel. "I don't want to get in trouble."

Rosemary rolled her eyes and said, "Please."

"OK, I have some change. She counted out $4.50 and handed it over. "See those snack machines over there. Live it up!"

Rosemary gave her a look that expressed more annoyance than gratitude, but she took the change and crossed the room. She came back with a bag of chips and a can of pop and didn't offer to share with Rachel or give her any change. Rachel wasn't even surprised at this point. She pulled out her mother's Bible and began searching for underlined verses to memorize.

The first verse that Rachel came upon was Galatians 6:30. "Therefore, as we have opportunity, let us do good to all people, especially to those who belong to the family of believers." Rachel said the verse over and over to herself until she knew it. It made her feel better to realize that she was taking care of Rosemary for the family; and they deserved it. *After all, they cared for me when I didn't have anyone else,* she thought. Rachel continued studying, and the time went by quickly. Finally they boarded the plane and headed north.

Rosemary sat on one side of Rachel, and a young boy sat on her other side. Rachel looked at him and said, "Hi. My name is Rachel. What's yours?"

"My name is Seth. Why?"

"Are you traveling alone?" asked Rachel. Rosemary looked bored and looked out the window.

"My aunt and uncle raised three kids and they all got married and had kids, and then they all disappeared. They are very sad, so Mom and Dad are sending me off to live with them for a while. They think they can handle me," said Seth.

"I see," said Rachel. "You are some kind of rebel."

"What of it?" asked Seth.

"Nothing," said Rachel. "It's just that I was a rebel myself."

"You aren't a rebel anymore?" Seth asked.

"Well, my parents disappeared," Rachel said. "I don't have anyone left to rebel against."

Seth looked at Rachel and didn't know what to say. He was probably wondering if it was that simple for him.

Rachel asked, "Did you ever read the Bible, Seth?"

"No. My parents wouldn't have a Bible in our house," Seth said.

"I thought you don't care what your parents think," said Rachel. "Why don't you get a Bible and read it."

"Being bad is a lot more fun," Seth said.

"Is this fun?" asked Rachel. "Being sent off to live with the relatives doesn't sound fun to me. I was never happy when my family all thought I was a freak. I don't know why I did it."

"So what are you going to do now?" asked Seth.

"I'm going home, and I'm going to get saved, and I'm going to live my life for Jesus from now on," Rachel answered. "Would you like to hear anything from the Bible Seth? I can start in the beginning in Genesis, or I could start with the birth of Christ. I bet your parents would be really mad if you read the Bible."

"I know you're trying to use reverse psychology on me," Seth said. "But you know, I would like to hear some of that. I don't even know what the Bible is about."

Rachel read the first two chapters of Genesis. Seth stopped her and asked, "Do you believe that God created the world in six days? My mom and dad think that people who believe that are ignorant. My parents are science teachers."

"No way," said Rachel. "My parents were science teachers too. They retired last year so they could go visit my brother and sister's families more and so they could go on mission trips a lot."

"So some science teachers believe that God created the world?" Seth asked.

"I guess so," said Rachel. "My parents taught me to believe that. I think I always believed in the creation. To me, it's a lot easier to believe that God created this beautiful world, the animals, the trees and flowers, the oceans and mountains, than it is to think it all happened accidentally."

"Will you keep reading?" asked Seth. "I never heard this stuff."

Rachel read and read and Seth seemed to be listening intently and he even seemed frustrated when she stopped to cough. Finally Rachel finished Genesis, chapter 4, that told about Adam and Eve having a son named Seth.

"Stop," said Seth. "Let me see that. Someone told me once that I have a Bible name."

Seth read aloud from her Bible. He read Genesis 4: 25 and 26. "Adam lay with his wife again, and she gave birth to a son and named him Seth, saying, 'God has granted me another child in place of Abel, since Cain killed him.' Seth also had a son, and he named him Enosh. At that time men began to call on the name of the Lord." Seth looked at Rachel. "This is good stuff. Where can I get my own Bible?"

"Anywhere," Rachel said. "I have several copies just lying around my house. By the way, where do your aunt and uncle live?"

Seth reached in his pocket and pulled out a paper

with an address and phone number on it, and showed it to Rachel.

"Canterbury Street," said Rachel. "You just might be one of my neighbors. Maybe your aunt and uncle can give me a lift to my house. I have two cars there, but they aren't at the airport."

"Do you think we can hang out sometime?" asked Seth. "After all, we are both rebels."

"You can hang out with me all you like," said Rachel, "but I have to warn you. I'm going to find a church that's operational, and that's where I'll be most of the time."

"I never went to church before, but from what I see on TV, it looks pretty boring," said Seth.

"Well churches will be different now," said Rachel, "since almost everyone in them disappeared."

"What are you talking about?" asked Seth.

"Don't you know?" asked Rachel. "Jesus came and took all his believers from all over the world to heaven? I guess it's going to get pretty bad here on earth, now, with all the Christians gone."

Seth look alarmed. "You're a believer," he said. "Why didn't he take you?"

"Well, I wasn't much of a Christian," said Rachel. "I hadn't been to church in a couple years, and I didn't pray or read the Bible."

"What do you mean that things are going to get pretty bad now?" Seth asked.

"Haven't you noticed that God is trying to wake us up?" asked Rachel. "Hurricanes, earthquakes, volcanos, floods. Not only that, but the world is getting a lot more evil without the Christians around. Haven't you watched the news lately?"

"I've kind of been in my own little video game world," Seth said.

Their plane landed and Rachel and Seth barely noticed. They walked out together, but Rachel was careful to keep Rosemary with them. Once they passed security, Seth's aunt and uncle came running up to him, and gave him a big hug. Seth introduced them to Rachel, and of course they knew her parents. But they were very upset when Rachel told them that they disappeared. Many of the people on the street were gone, and they didn't know what was going to happen to their neighborhood.

Rachel and Rosemary just listened as Seth's aunt and uncle drove them home. They were scared out of their minds by the things like the disappearances and now all of the natural disasters. Seth's aunt had a coworker living with them, because she lost her home to the northeast Ohio sludge. Seth's Uncle Gordon's parents were in a tornado last night and they were coming to live with them too.

"I'm so sorry Seth," said his aunt. "We were planning to give you your own room, and for now, you'll have to sleep in the den on a sofa.

"That's ok, really Aunt Kathy," said Seth. "I'll try not to be any trouble." His aunt and uncle looked at each other. Rachel guessed that they were expecting Seth to be very difficult.

"Aunt Kathy, do you have a Bible I can use?" asked Seth. "I've decided to read it."

Seth's uncle looked surprised and said, "That's the same thing my dad asked me. They forgot to take their Bible to the basement when the tornado hit. He was sorrier about losing his Bible than his gun collection that was worth a lot of money."

"That's how I would feel if I lost my Bible," Rachel said.

The family pulled into Rachel's driveway and she and Rosemary got out. Rachel pulled out her keys and they went inside.

"Make yourself at home while I make us a little lunch," said Rachel. After they ate, Rachel said, "I really need a little nap before we go over to Jesse's."

"I'll just go outside and stretch my legs," said Rosemary.

"That's ok," said Rachel. "I have you back in Ohio now, so if you get lost, I'm not looking for you."

Rosemary laughed and said, "Don't worry. I'll stay in the yard."

Rachel went to her bedroom and nothing ever looked so good to her. In the past, why didn't she recognize the special things her parents did for her? Suddenly Rachel was overwhelmed with sorrow and tears ran down her cheeks. "Lord, forgive me for my sins. I was a rebellious teen and I didn't appreciate the wonderful things my parents did for me or the blessings you sent my way." She crawled on her bed and covered up with her mom's wrap up and went sound asleep. When she woke up, Rosemary was sitting in the family room watching TV.

"Rosemary, would you like to go over to Jesse's house now and see what's going on with your family?" Rachel asked. Rosemary nodded and got up and soon they were heading to their house.

"It quit raining," said Rosemary. "I was really disappointed to come back to Ohio after sitting on that sunny beach."

Rachel said a silent prayer, "Lord help me. Please let her family be there, so I can safely turn her over to them. And, please, help me find a church. In Jesus' name, Amen."

CHAPTER TWENTY-THREE

The family pulled into Jesse's driveway, with Ken and Lori in their car and Josh, Matt, and Larry in the grandparents' car. To their surprise, Rachel and Rosemary followed them in. They all hugged and watched as the rainbow faded. They stood in the driveway for a while.

"I'm so sorry that I cut Rosemary's vacation short, but I am really short on cash," said Rachel.

"We're relieved to have you back safe and sound. We wanted to communicate, but we haven't had working phones for days," said Matt. The whole family looked at Rosemary, trying to decide if she was up to the news that their home was gone.

"Wow Mom," said Lori. "Look at your tan! Did you have fun?"

Rosemary grinned and pulled down her shirt at the neck to show her tan shoulder. "I had fun at the beach, but I don't think Rachel did."

"No, I got stung by a jellyfish," said Rachel. "I never want to go through that again."

All of a sudden, a very sleepy Jesse appeared at the front door. The family walked up to the house and asked if they could come in for a visit. Jesse looked more grown up than they remembered. He looked like his mom, except for dark hair like his dad's. Jesse shook hands with Matt, Josh, Ken, and Larry, and took a big hug from Lori. They introduced Rachel to Jesse and explained that she drove Stephanie's car home from college, since Stephanie and almost everyone from that college disappeared.

"So, Stephanie did disappear!" said Jesse. "Her car creeped me out a little. I kept expecting her to come around the corner."

Jesse fixed everyone an iced tea, and they all sat down to visit. Matt began his confession to Jesse that he had been thinking about for a few days. "I guess you probably know by now that we were here right after the disappearances. We thought your whole family was gone. We lived in your house, drove your cars, ate your food, and took your money. I just want to say that we are really sorry, and it will take a while, but we'll try and pay you back. Had we known that you were alive, we wouldn't have done that."

"Uncle Matt. Please don't worry about it," said Jesse. "It's over and done. I took a couple of days and got my affairs in order. I sold my dad's store, and I closed their bank accounts, and I got rid of the extra cars. Seriously, don't worry about it. I'm thankful that I still have family alive."

"Lori, do you want to tell them about last night?" asked Matt.

Lori looked at her mom and hesitated. Rosemary asked, "What happened Lori?"

"Ken and I were at your house with Dad and Larry," Lori said. "Then we all woke up in the night. We went to the basement, and a tornado hit. The house and the barn and most of the trees are gone. You wouldn't recognize the place. Everything is gone but the basement."

Rosemary surprised everyone with her reaction. "I didn't like the place much anyway. We still own the land, don't we? We can build a new house."

Matt looked kind of sad, and said, "Well, we don't have any homeowners insurance. Maybe the governor could declare a state of emergence and give us some money, but considering the state of the world, we won't count on it."

"My place was wiped out too, Jesse, the day of the disappearances," said Josh. "Some kind of plane went through there. It even wiped out the store I worked in, so I don't even have a job."

"This is really embarrassing, but basically Rosemary and I and Josh and Larry are homeless, although some of us could live at Mom and Dad's house," said Matt. "We don't have jobs and we are almost all out of money."

"Lori and I still have our apartment," said Ken. "We haven't gone back to our jobs, because we were thinking about settling near here. We were hoping you could put us up for a little while, Jesse."

Before Jesse could say anything, Rachel spoke up. "Oh please Lori, I would love it if you and Ken came to live at my house. I have tons of room, and I don't want to be alone. You guys could have Mom and Dad's room."

"That would be great, Rachel," said Lori. "We could get jobs around here and help with the expenses."

"Larry and I can live at Grandma and Grandpa's house," said Josh. "But for some strange reason, we have felt drawn to this area. It's like there is something here we are supposed to do."   Finally Jesse spoke up. "Remember when I said that I got my affairs in order? Well, before I got my finances in order, I took care of something far more important, and that was my spiritual condition. I went to church on Sunday morning. There were twelve of us there, and we all made our confession of faith that Jesus Christ died for us, and that he is God's son. And then we all were baptized."

Everyone started to talk at once, saying that was what they wanted to do too. They all kind of laughed."

"If you want to be baptized, we can go over to the church right now and take care of that," said Jesse. "I'll call my friends and see if they can join us."

Jesse made a couple of calls and made sure that Danny could open the building for them. Rachel wanted to stop off at her house and get some extra clothes to change into, so she got directions to the church. Josh asked if he could go with her, and they left together. Josh waited in the car while Rachel ran in for her clothes. While he was sitting there, a kid ran up to the house and knocked. Rachel opened the door and talked for a minute, and then she and the kid walked to the car.

"Seth is a boy I met on the plane, and it turns out that he's my neighbor. He's going with us to the church," said Rachel.

They all went to the church and moved to the front where Jesse and his friends sang on Sunday. Will and Andrew arrived and they sang a praise song as Jesse played the piano. Matt's family and Rachel and Seth didn't know the words, but they listened with fascination. Will read Luke 15:7. "I tell you that in the same way there will be more rejoicing in heaven over one sinner who repents than over ninety-nine righteous persons who do not need to repent."

"So who wants to be baptized?" asked Andrew. Ken and Lori looked at each other and raised their hands. Matt and Larry and Josh and Rachel all raised their hands.

Seth spoke out loud. "Hey, I want to get baptized too. I just read the whole book of John, and even though I haven't seen Jesus, I believe in him."

Matt looked at Rosemary and asked her, "Don't you want to get baptized?"

"No," said Rosemary. "Where did this come from? I don't remember discussing this."

"Well, we've been planning this since the first night in the hotel. I guess you were kind of asleep," said Matt. "You can just watch tonight and wait until you are ready."

So the seven of them were baptized, and Jesse, Will, and Andrew were excited to see their church growing. They planned to return tomorrow night for Bible study.

Jesse knew that the family was kind of down and out, and he didn't want to embarrass them or hurt their pride. "How about if I pick up pizza for everyone and we all go to my house for a celebration?" Jesse said.

"I have plenty of soft drinks at my house," said Rachel. "I'll stop by and get some and check with Seth's aunt and uncle to see if he can join us."

Will, Andrew, and Danny, the church custodian said they would pick up some chips and come too. Matt, Rosemary, Ken, Lori, and Larry arrived at the house long before Jesse, who was picking up the pizza. This time they had no way to get into the house, so they walked around the yard.

"This was where I was going to plant some roses," said Rosemary. "Now all my plans are ruined since Jesse

Boy is still here."

"I'm glad he's here," said Matt. "He's such a good boy, and he's all alone in the world."

They wandered around the yard for most of an hour and then everyone began rolling in. Finally Jesse arrived with a tall stack of pizzas, and let the group in. They stood around the kitchen and had a prayer, and began to eat. Jesse received two long phone calls, so he joined everyone long after they finished eating.

Jesse looked at his watch a couple times as he talked nervously. He looked around at the group like he was analyzing everyone. He seemed to look at Seth for a long time.

Rachel noticed and said, "This is Seth. I know he's younger than the rest of us, but he is a Christian now."

"I need to share something with all of you, because I'm going to need your help. But you have to know that what I'm going to tell you must be kept a secret," Jesse said. Then he checked his watch again.

"I'm all alone," said Danny the custodian. "I don't have anyone to tell a secret to."

"I can keep a secret," said Seth. Everyone else encouraged Jesse to tell them what is going on.

"OK," said Jesse. "I'm going to begin by telling you about my day at school. There is a group of kids at school, called the Pythons, who dress all in black and are mean and intimidating. They were there before my accident and the disappearances, but now they are more aggressive and dangerous."

"Oh no," said Lori. "Please be careful Jesse."

"Well, I just got a call from one of them, a guy named Tim Davenport," said Jesse. "He used to be a friend of mine on the swim team. He said that he joined the Pythons because he was bored and because they made him feel tough and important. Ever since the disappearances, the group has been taking some drug and alcohol combination that makes them crazy. Tim says he has been pretending to take the drugs because they will kill him if he doesn't do what they want. I'm leaving now to pick him up in a secluded location, and he's going to just drop out of sight."

Jesse moved toward the door and several started to stop him. Jesse's friend Andrew said what they were all thinking. "Hold on, Jesse. This could be a setup. Maybe they are actually planning to attack you."

"You have a big SUV. We guys will all go with you. If it's a setup, we'll be prepared," said Will.

Danny pulled out a gun and said, "I'm prepared. You'll be glad to have me along." The group looked shocked and stared at him. "Oh, I live in a very dangerous neighborhood. I have a permit to carry this gun."

"Let's go," said Jesse. "I don't want him standing out there all alone very long." He grabbed his keys and headed for the door. Andrew, Will, Danny, Larry, and Josh all followed him. Mat and Ken would have gone along, but they didn't think there would be enough seats in the car. Seth wanted to go, but Rachel held him back.

As the guys were traveling to the meeting place, Andrew asked Jesse who the second call was from. "Oh, Tim Davenport was the second call," said Jesse. "The first call was from a teacher at my school. I don't know him, but he told me that he is a new Christian and that if I need any help, I can go to him. The teacher said that for now, he is going to keep his faith a secret. Since the Christians were taken away, the school is a dangerous place. He warned me to watch my back, since everyone knows I'm Christian."

The guys drove about fifteen minutes and turned down a quiet alley. Tim had a description of the SUV, so he came out of hiding when he saw it. He was wearing a blue hooded sweatshirt and jeans. His head was covered by the hood, and he held it close around his face. Jesse rolled down his window to make sure that it was Tim, and then told him to get in the car.

"If the Pythons find me, I'm a dead man. I wish I could just leave town, better yet the country," said Tim. "Do you think you guys could shave my hair off? I never want to have black hair again."

"Do you really think those guys are capable of murder?" asked Jesse.

"Absolutely," said Tim. "They killed two people last week. Did you read in the paper about the homeless guys in the city who died last week? It looked like they died of natural causes, but I know for a fact that they were killed by four members of our gang, and they did it for kicks. They get more violent every day, and I'm afraid that I'm the next one to die of 'natural causes.' They have been questioning my allegiance to the group because I resist joining in their evil deeds. They've been stealing too, to pay for drugs. I saw them knock around one guy's grandfather when he wouldn't buy their liquor for them. They are in to other things, too, that I don't want to talk about. Do you know any way I could move away? I would be much safer."

"Tim, do you have any family left?" asked Jesse.

"Oh, sure," said Tim. "They are all still at the house. They kicked me out last year, but I know they are still around. I saw them out in the yard picking up sticks after all that rain."

"Don't you want them to know that you left the group?" asked Josh. "And don't you want them to know that you are still alive?"

"No," said Tim. "That could put them in danger. I'll let them know later, if things get better."

The guys arrived at the house and pulled into the garage. They closed the garage door before getting Tim out of the car. Inside the house, they closed all the blinds and curtains.

Tim gave them all a warning. "Be very careful not to tell the cops about the stuff I told you tonight about the Pythons. You can't trust them anymore. Believe me, in this town, they are all crooked now."

Jesse gave Tim a bedroom upstairs and Tim told him that he will get the first good night's sleep in a very long time.

Will, Andrew, and Danny all left, discussing moving in together, and whether Will should return to school. Andrew told him not to do it, because his school was just as dangerous as Jesse's. The only reason Andrew was going to school now was to bring students to church.

Lori said to Rachel, "If the offer for us to move into your house is still there, Ken and I want to take you up on it. We promise to look for jobs tomorrow and help with the expenses."

"I really need the company and the support," said Rachel. "Let's get going, because I need to get Seth home."

"Before you go, let's all have a prayer together," said Jesse. First of all, they prayed for Jesse's safely at school the next day, and that Tim can remain hidden. Then they prayed that the family could find jobs in the area.

Jesse gave Matt and Rosemary his mom and dad's room, Larry Jamie's room, and Josh the room with the crib and toys. Jesse thought that today was the longest, most exhausting day of his life. He went to bed, completely wiped out, but no longer alone in the world.

CHAPTER TWENTY-FOUR

Wednesday, Day Nine

Jesse got up Wednesday morning when his alarm went off and he headed for the shower. He could see two people talking quietly in the shadows of the family room, so he went to check it out. Josh was listening to Tim. They looked startled to see someone coming, but they were relieved to see Jesse.

"Hey Jesse," said Josh. "What do you think of my barber skills? I found some hair coloring in Aunt Melinda's bathroom."

Jesse looked at Tim, who had a nice haircut. His hair was sandy blond and he was wearing glasses. "I wouldn't have recognized you Tim," said Jesse. "Does that make you feel safer?"

"I won't feel safer until I'm in another city. Josh promised to take me to his grandparents' house in a couple of days," said Tim.

"Well I have to go back and take care of the cats soon anyway, so I thought maybe Tim could stay there and take care of Grandma's cats," said Josh. "And then maybe I could stay here for a while."

"That's actually a really good idea, Josh," said Jesse. "But you had better take really good care of Grandma and Grandpa's house and their cats, Tim. How are you going to have money to live on? What about your ID? Those guys can trace you and find you?

"I can get a new driver's license and use my middle name, and then get a new bank account," said Tim. "About money, I'll get a job. I'll work in a Home Depot or something. I love that stuff."

"Why don't you take him there today, Josh?" asked Jesse. "Sooner is better."

"I was going out job hunting since I barely have any money," said Josh. "I can't even buy gas. And I have to ask Dad if I can take Grandma and Grandpa's car."

"I have enough money to pay for the whole trip," said Tim. "My parents are pretty well off. The Pythons don't know about that. They put money in a checking account for me, and since I don't spend much, they never cut me off. I got out one hundred dollars yesterday, knowing I was going underground, but I'll never use that account again. And I broke my cell phone before you picked me up last night."

"Great," said Josh. "Would you pay for Rachel to go along too? We will need lunch?"

"The girl with the kid?" asked Tim.

"Yes," said Josh. "He's just her neighbor kid."

"That's fine," said Tim. "I'm going to get cleaned up and ready to go. I feel better already."

"I have to get ready for school," said Jesse. "Have a safe trip. If you have enough gas, get out of town before you fill up."

Jesse was soon walking into school. When he entered

the library, he thought he must be in the wrong place. The room was full of students.

"Jesse, we took a head count and there are twenty-three of us today, counting you. I'm Adam, helping out," he said.

"Where did all these kids come from?" Jesse asked.

One of the new girls overheard and spoke to Jesse. "Hi. Most of us heard your invitation to Bible study yesterday, and we just kind of laughed it off. But we were scared all day as the Pythons pushed us around."

"OK," said Jesse. "But how did you know to come in the morning?"

The girl held up a pink slip of paper. On it was the following message: Are you afraid to go to school? *Then join us for prayer and support each morning before school in the main library. The Remnant.*

"Where did you get this?" asked Jesse.

"I can explain," said Victoria. "Since Mrs. Jenkins, the librarian, disappeared, I've been running the library, and no one seems to care. So I have access to all the supplies. I made the invitations last night after I saw a few Pythons giving some guys a drink they called power tea. I don't know what's in that stuff, but after they drank it, they got a crazed look in their eyes. I think the Pythons are recruiting members that way, so I thought, for safety, we should do some recruiting too. I made up flyers and slipped them to students this morning- students who I thought look more like us than like them."

"Good thinking," said Jesse. Then he raised his voice and said to the group, "As you know, since the disappearances, evil in the world seems to be growing rapidly. It's not safe to walk through the halls of our own school. At the same time, God calls out to us, to catch our attention, by hurricanes, earthquakes, volcanoes, and even the northeast Ohio sludge. All of us missed the safe passage to heaven with Jesus that our friends and family had when they disappeared. I lost my whole family and my girlfriend Beth. But we are not going to give up. Last Sunday I returned to my own church. There were just a handful of us left, but we confessed our faith in Jesus Christ, baptized each other, and committed ourselves to living for him. If any of you would like to join us, tonight is our first Wednesday night Bible study at 7 PM. Pick up directions on your way out. But now, gather in a large circle for prayer. Do any of you have urgent prayer requests?"

A girl from Jesse's math class raised her hand and spoke, "Last night, our house shook all night. We live up north, just beyond the airport. My mom and dad think the sludge is going to move again. I couldn't sleep all night for fear of being buried alive."

Another girl raised her hand. "Some Pythons live near my house. They tripped my grandma on the sidewalk the other day, and then laughed at her as she tried to get up. We're scared to leave the house."

A boy raised his hand. "The Pythons actually offered me a drink of some brown liquid yesterday. They told me that it would make me strong and smart, and that by drinking it, I could train to become one of them. I told them that I wasn't thirsty. The look they gave me was frightening. I felt like they were following me around the rest of the day."

One more girl raised her hand. "This is really hard to say out loud. I don't think my mom disappeared because she was here after the disappearances. But she hasn't come home since last Saturday, and our neighbor guy found out and now he stops in to check on me and my sister a lot. I don't like the way he looks at us. He's been getting a little too affectionate, if you know what I mean. Could you pray for us please?"

"Of course," said Jesse. A few more students were raising their hands, but Jesse said, "I'm sorry, but we barely have time left to pray. Victoria, can you make up a sheet of prayer requests?"

She nodded her head that she could, and then Jesse said, "Let's pray."

The students all reached out and held hands in a large prayer circle. Jesse began, "Dear Lord, many of us here are in desperate situations but we have the promise that you will never forsake those who seek you. And we are seeking your help and your comfort. Keep us safe and let us help each other as well. In Jesus' name we pray. Amen."

The bell rang and many rushed off to class. Jesse sent kids who wanted to talk over to Victoria and he ducked out the door. He went to American Government class first. He expected it to be easy, since there weren't any Pythons in there, but he was mistaken. The teacher called him Prayer Boy and mocked him all period. Students who used to be his friends laughed along with everyone else.

When the bell rang, Jesse went out into the hall, and ran into Larry. "What are you doing here at my school?" asked Jesse.

"Well, I needed a job, and I thought of working as a custodian," said Larry. "So Josh dropped me off here this morning on his way out of town. But they took one look at me and hired me on the spot for security. I guess they get a lot of complaints from parents who say their kids are scared at school. So my job is to protect the good students from the bad students. I start right away and can just wear these clothes until my uniform comes in. Look, they gave me a cell phone so they can reach me any time and any place."

"Watch out for yourself," warned Jesse. "There are some dangerous characters around here."

Jesse went through his day, avoiding the Pythons whenever he saw them in the hall. He stopped in the library once and got a copy of the prayer request sheet from Victoria. It was two pages long and quite overwhelming. These poor students were going to need more support than a morning-prayer session.

Jesse went home to an empty house. There was a note from Matt on the kitchen counter. It read, "Jesse, Josh dropped Larry off at a school to apply for a job. He took Tim and Rachel to Grandma and Grandpa's so he can care for the cats and hide out. Lori and Ken are taking Rosemary and me out job hunting. Here is your mother's cell phone. We tried to charge it up, but it doesn't seem to have any service. Uncle Matt."

Jesse smiled when he read it. He shut off the cell phone service the day he got his finances in order. Jesse decided to call Andrew and plan tonight's Bible study.

"Hey Andrew," said Jesse. "I think we're going to have quite a few students attending tonight."

"That's great," said Andrew. "I have exciting news too. Will and Danny moved in with me this morning, and then we went to the church and baptized Danny." They talked a while about the lesson for that night and hung up.

Then the family came home. Lori and Ken got jobs at the local Walmart without any trouble. They told Jesse that they were working Monday through Friday, daytime hours.

"I thought you didn't like working at Walmart," said Jesse.

Lori answered, "That was just a job. Now we are working for the Lord. We will look for opportunities to serve him at work and when we aren't at work."

"I got a job too," said Matt. "I will work at the hospital, cleaning and sanitizing rooms when people check out. Then I get the rooms ready for the next patients. It's good, honest work, and I'm looking forward to it."

"What did you do back at your home, Uncle Matt?" asked Jesse.

"I hated that job," said Matt. "I was a used car salesman. I got special bonuses for moving certain cars. Some of them were stolen and some had things wrong with them. Some were flooded. I couldn't sleep at night. I could never buy one of those cars for myself. When Mom and Dad and Sydney and everyone else disappeared, I just didn't go back."

"Did you get a job too, Aunt Rosemary?" asked Jesse.

Matt answered for her. "No. Rosemary doesn't really work. She likes to keep busy at home."

"Are you going to cook and clean for us?" asked Jesse.

"I'll cook one meal a day, at dinner time," said Rosemary. "I don't like to clean much, but I pick up after myself. Josh, Larry, and Matt will clean the house and do the dishes after the meal I cook."

Jesse didn't know what to say. Finally Matt said, "As soon as I get my first paycheck, I'll shop and get the food. I did that back home."

The family sat down in the kitchen. Jesse pulled out the prayer request sheet that Victoria had prepared. He read the requests out loud, and the family was speechless.

Finally Matt said, "I guess we can't feel too sorry for ourselves. We don't have those kind of problems."

"No, but I think we can do more than pray for these kids," said Lori. "Look here. This girl and her sister live alone and are scared of some weird neighbor guy. This family is afraid the sludge is going to wipe out their house. They could move in with the two girls, temporarily of course, and for a while, they are all safer. Their phone numbers are here. Should I go call them?"

"Go for it!" said Jesse.

Lori went in the other room and made the calls. She came back and said, "The sludge is coming out of the ground again and moving south. The family is packing their car right now to leave and they could use some help. I called those two girls and they love the idea of the family coming to stay with them. Let's go help them with their stuff."

"Does that mean your house is in danger, Jesse?" asked Matt.

"Maybe eventually," said Jesse. "We can check it out as we help them move."

Matt got in the car with Ken and Lori. Lori handed Jesse a copy of the address and he backed out of his driveway. He saw his neighbor Brook, who ran up to the car.

"What's going on?" Brook asked. "Your family took off like the house was on fire."

"Something like that," said Jesse. "The sludge is moving again and getting near a family from school. We are going to help them move some of their stuff."

"Can I come along and help?" Brook asked.

She got in and went along. When they arrived, there were many emergency vehicles around. They were evacuating the area and setting up roadblocks.

"Would you look at that," said Brook. "That's the sludge, right over there."

"Weird," said Jesse. "It looks like a black lake."

"Yes, and it smells kind of funny too," said Brook.

Jesse put all the seats down in his SUV. The man of the house came out and shook hands with Jesse.

"I can't thank you enough for helping us move, and for setting it up for us to help those girls. My name is Frankie Jones," the man said. "It looks like you have room there for a few pieces of furniture. I'll show you which ones. We aren't taking much." Jesse and Brook worked quickly, along with Matt, Lori, and Ken. Soon they were heading for the girls' house, along with Mr. Jones and his wife and two daughters.

While the family was gone, Will, Andrew, and Danny arrived at Jesse's house to prepare for tonight's Bible study. Rosemary told them that Jesse was gone, moving a family. She was going to shut the door, but they asked if they could come in and study until he gets home. Rosemary let them in and went in the other room and turned on the TV. She saw coverage of the sludge and realized how close it was to them. She could feel panic rising in her throat and thought she was going to barf. She thought, *we should just get in the car and go home. We can stay at Matt's parents' house until we can rebuild ours.*

The family came running in around 6:00 pm. "We have just enough time to eat and get to Bible study," said

Jesse. "What's for dinner Aunt Rosemary."

Rosemary looked at him like he was crazy. "What, we're just going to eat and go to Bible study, like everything is all right?"

"Well it is dinner time, and you did say you'd cook it every night, and serve it at six," said Matt. "It's six now."

"That was before the sludge started moving again," she answered. "I figured we would pack up and head south."

"We might have to," said Matt. "But it's not that close yet."

"Well let's all go to Taco Bell on the way to the church," said Jesse.

"Oh, we don't have any money yet," said Matt.

"It's on me," said Jesse.

Just then Josh and Rachel walked in, back from taking Tim to Grandma and Grandpa's house. "Tim's all settled in," said Josh. "I gave him a key, so he can go to the store or the library. And he loves cats. I didn't expect that."

Then Larry arrived, exhausted, but happy to go with them to Bible study.

"I asked Brook next door to go with us to Bible study, but she said she's not ready for that," said Jesse.

"Well, if you don't mind, I don't think I'll go either," said Rosemary.

"If you want to eat, you'll come along," said Matt. Rosemary frowned and grabbed her jacket and walked out the door.

They all went to Taco Bell, ate, and arrived at church a few minutes early. This time there were lots of students from school, plus all of the people who were baptized with Jesse. The elderly couple, Earl and Wilma, arrived, as well as Terry Harold and his wife, who bought the pharmacy from Jesse. They decided to divide into two groups, since Will and Andrew were both prepared to lead. Danny watched the front door until people stopped arriving, then he locked the door and joined the study.

The guys decided at dinner that Andrew and Jesse would take all of the high school students in their group and Will would take all of the adults. Although Larry was an adult, he went in with the high school group, since he would be in school every day for his job.

Just as the groups were beginning, an explosion rocked the building. Some of the tiles fell from the ceiling, so Danny took off to check the place for damage. Both groups decided to go ahead and have their studies and find out later what caused the earth-shaking sound.

Andrew began by saying, "I believe that we are facing a very dangerous time, in our schools and out of our schools. There are some very evil people in the world today, and it's getting more and more difficult to avoid them. We need to be prepared to resist those who would like to harm us. Let's turn to Ephesians 6:10 and begin there."

Andrew read, "Finally be strong in the Lord and in his mighty power. Put on the full armor of God so that you can take your stand against the devil's schemes. For our struggle is not against flesh and blood, but against the rulers, against the authorities, against the powers of this dark world and against the spiritual forces of evil in the heavenly realms." Andrew could see everyone squirming in their seats. "Do you guys have any questions?" he asked.

"I put up a good front," said Victoria, "but I'm afraid all of the time. I'm pretty comfortable in the library because the Pythons aren't exactly book lovers, but when I have to go out to class, I shake all over. I only have my dad at home, since my mom and three sisters all disappeared."

"I would like to read another verse for you all to think about," said Andrew. "This is from I Thessalonians 5:16. 'Be joyful always; pray continually; give thanks in all circumstances, for this is God's will for you in Christ Jesus.'"

"I have a question," said one of the girls. "How can I possibly be thankful when I just lost my whole family, and I am stuck in that big house all alone, and I have no idea how to pay the bills or take care of things? And now I have to worry about sludge drowning me in the night."

"You can't think of one thing to be thankful for?" asked Andrew.

"OK, if it's true that my family went to heaven, then I'm happy for them," she said in a slightly sarcastic way.

"At first I was pretty upset that my family all went there without me," said Jesse. "But then I got to thinking that all of my loved ones are in the safest place of all- with God. So all I have to do is get there too. That's all I'm focusing on now, just getting to heaven and taking a few people with me."

Just then Danny came running in and said, "You might want to turn on Channel 8, and check out that explosion." He went over and turned on the TV.

The TV anchorman looked very serious as he spoke. "About fifteen minutes ago our area was rocked as a geyser bigger than Old Faithful was released near the sight known as the northeast Ohio sludge. The geyser appears to contain a thick, black substance, and it is pouring onto our land at an increasing rate. Right now, all of the aircraft at the Akron/Canton Airport are taking off in an effort to save the equipment, and all employees were told to depart. Residents in that vicinity are to drive south immediately, taking only essentials. People without transportation should call 911, and a rescue vehicle will come and get you."

Several of the students were showing signs of panic. One girl passed out and fell on the floor, and another girl was having a panic attack. Andrew was very calm as he reassured the group. "We're safe here," he said. "I would say this church is miles from the airport. How many of you live up near the airport in the area that's being evacuated?" Two of the students raised their hands. One of them was the girl who passed out.

"Do you have family members at home?" Jesse asked.

The guy who raised his hand said that he had a mom and two brothers and that he should probably get home and get them out of town.

"Do you have a place to go?" asked Jesse.

"No, I don't think so. My grandparents aren't answering their phone and my aunt can't get in their house," he said. "They live out of state anyway."

"For now, your family can come to my house, but we don't know how long it will be safe," said Jesse. "Then he looked at the girl who fainted. "What about you? Oh I remember you are like me and lost your whole family."

"As far as I know, I don't have grandparents or aunts or uncles or even a cousin," said the girl. "I'm only fifteen, so they'll probably make me go to a foster home. Please will you help me get some stuff out of my house? It's all I have left of my family."

Jesse stood up and said, "Andrew, will you tell my

family that I left without them? They can get a ride home with Lori and Ken.

"I got it," said Larry. "I'll let the family know that we are all riding together and that we need to pick up snacks and find blankets, pillows, and towels for sleep-over visitors. Hopefully one of us will have some money."

Jesse stopped and handed Larry a twenty dollar bill. Then he headed for the door with the guy and two girls following him. "Why are you following me?" Jesse asked the one girl who, although was left alone, did not live near the evacuation area.

"If it's all right with you," she said, "I'll come along and help move them out. My car will hold a lot of stuff. Maybe I can stay with you tonight, and then if there's a nice family who needs a place to live, they can move in with me."

"That's a good idea," said Jesse. "Follow me."

The fifteen-year-old girl headed for a car in the parking Lot. "Where are you going?" Jesse called to her.

"I'm going to my car," she answered. "Well I've been driving pretty well and no one has noticed that I look too young."

"Leave the car here for now." said Jesse. "It will be safer here in the church parking lot."

She looked a little annoyed, but got in the car with Jesse. The guy with the mom and two brothers pulled out first, followed by Jesse, and then the other girl who was left alone.

CHAPTER TWENTY-FIVE

Will's group was not in a panic like Andrew's group. No one lived in the evacuation area, and since they were all adults, no one was facing danger in the schools. Matt noticed that Rosemary didn't come into the classroom with him, but he wasn't really surprised. He figured she would just wander around the building and find something to do. He probably should have just let her stay home.

Will's group had the same lesson on the Armor of God that the other class had, but they read a lot more scripture and had many good discussions.

Will asked, "How can we wear the belt of truth and the breastplate of righteousness?"

"I think that we need to tell the truth in all circumstances and try to do the right thing," said Ken.

"OK," said Will. "How can we have our feet fitted with readiness that comes from the gospel of truth?"

Earl answered, "I think we need to read our Bibles more than ever before, and in order to be ready, we need to stay focused, and not get distracted by the things of this world."

"And do you think it will be easier to resist the things of this world now or harder than before the disappearances?" asked Will.

"I think it will be easier by far to resist them now," said Wilma.

"How so?" asked Will.

"Because before the disappearances, evil was subtle. Now evil is easy to recognize. Now evil is ugly and frightful," Wilma answered.

"Well we know the truth about Jesus now and how we missed out," said Will. "But there are plenty of people now who are attracted to the evil things. Just look at the TV these days."

Danny came running into their class this time, just like he did Andrew's. "There is an urgent phone call for Jesse, but he left a while ago to rescue some folks from the sludge. Do any of you want to take the call? It's from his neighbor Brook."

"Oh, I know Brook. I'll take the call," said Lori. She followed Danny into the office and picked up the phone. "Hello, Brook. This is Lori. Jesse had to leave early."

Lori listened intently for a few minutes and then she said, "I don't know how to reach him right now, but I'll try. Are you safe where you are?" Lori listened a while longer and then said, "We'll be careful. Thanks for the warning."

Lori walked back into Bible study, and everyone stopped and looked at her curiously. She began, "Our neighbor Brook called. She looked out of her backyard window and saw guys dressed in black sneaking through our backyard and around our house. She counted seven of them. One stayed outside to stand guard, and the others went in. Brook said she wished she had a way to listen to them, and then she remembered the baby monitor. She was best friends with Amy. Amy had a baby monitor in her room and would turn it on sometimes when she wanted to give Brook a message, and then Brook would raise and lower her window blind to answer. Anyway, Brook turned on the receiver, and the monitor was still turned on in Amy's room. She listened in on those guys. They are out to get Jesse because of the prayer meetings he's having at school. She said to be careful of the food and drinks, because they left some kind of drug in the house.

"Wow!" said Josh. "What if you would have let Mom stay home? Anything could have happened to her." Matt looked very serious.

Josh and Rachel looked at each other. They had the same thought. *What if they had waited until tomorrow to take Tim to Grandma and Grandpa's house? He would probably be dead by now.* They didn't say anything because they promised not to mention Tim to anyone for a while.

"Should we call the police?" asked Matt.

Everyone there said, "NO." All the cops in Canton are crooked now.

Will stood up again and asked, "Is there anyone here who would like to accept Christ as their personal savior and be baptized?"

Earl and Wilma and Terry Harold and his wife all raised their hands, as well as three others in the adult group. In the hallway outside the classroom, there were quite a few teens standing around talking. Will told them that they were headed to the worship center for baptisms and they were welcome to join them. The teens turned and followed them and more than twenty people were baptized that night.

Matt wanted to watch the baptisms, but he was a worried about Rosemary, since she hadn't been seen for over an hour. He started wandering around the church building and finally found her curled up on a sofa in a little room, probably someone's office. She was asleep, with her arms wrapped tightly across her chest. Her eyes were red and puffy, evidence that she had been crying.

"What's the matter, Honey?" Matt asked.

"I'm so scared. Can't we just get in the car and go home?" Rosemary asked. "I don't want to drown in sludge." Matt realized that she didn't even know about Brook's call about the Pythons. She might really freak out when she hears about that.

"Don't you realize that there isn't a safe place to go?" asked Matt. "There are bad people everywhere. God is trying to draw us to him, and keep us aware of him through events, like the hurricane and earthquakes and tornados and even the sludge. If you want to be safe, you need to put your life in his hands. The rest of us have accepted Christ. What about you?"

Rosemary's face changed immediately from fear to defiance. "That is what I married you for- to take care of me and keep me safe. Now keep me safe! Get me out of this mud-flowing town. There isn't anything here for us now. He sold all the cars and closed the accounts. He even stopped Melinda's phone service. And now I'm expected to cook and clean for everyone. Well forget it! I want to go home, where I might not have much, but at least my time is my own."

"I like our life here," said Matt. "I have a job where I can help people. And I love this church. We have more friends here in just a few days than we had back home in all those years. And most important to me is that Jesse needs us."

"It's more like we need him," said Rosemary.

"There are people coming to the house tonight because they have no place else to go," said Matt. "I want to be there to comfort them. Don't you feel like we are finally living?"

"I felt like I was living when I was sitting on a beach. Now that was living! Couldn't we sell our property and go down there and rent a little place near the ocean? There are hospitals everywhere that you can work in," said Rosemary.

"There is no way that Lori or Josh would leave now," said Matt. "They love it here."

"Well, they can come visit us for Thanksgiving or Christmas," said Rosemary.

"Do you honestly think we would be safe there?" asked Matt. "No place is safe! And yet somehow I feel safe now that my life is in God's hands."

CHAPTER TWENTY-SIX

When Jesse and his caravan arrived in the evacuation area, he couldn't believe how much worse the situation was than a couple hours earlier. He could actually see the geyser and the lake of sludge in the distance. The air was filled with a strange odor and a dirty mist. Since the guy named Nick, had a mom and two brothers waiting for them, Jesse had to go there first. He had the girl with him get in the other girl's car.

Nick's mom was so relieved to see them. "Mom," Nick said. "This is my new friend Jesse from school, and he's going to let us move in with him for now. Let's get out of here."

Nick's mom instructed the two younger boys to take their stuff to the garage and get in the car and stay there. She told Nick that he had five minutes to gather as many of his favorite things and get to the car. Then she asked Jesse to help her carry out her pile. Jesse told her that she can fill his car too. She was overjoyed. She showed him a few more things to carry out. In a matter of minutes the family was ready to leave. Jesse gave Nick directions to his house, and let him drive his car there.

Jesse got in the car with the two girls and they drove

to the other evacuation area. He could hardly believe the size of her house or the wealth of her neighborhood. "By the way, what are your names?" Jesse asked.

"I'm Debra and this is Heather," she said. Debra led them into a very impressive house.

"How can you possible choose what to save?" asked Heather. "Everything looks valuable."

"I may be young, but I'm not stupid," Debra said. "I've been watching the news very carefully and I've already selected and packaged everything to save." She took Jesse and Heather to the garage, where there were three vehicles. "I have all my mom's jewelry and pretty clothes in the trunk of the Lexus, with my clothes, books, and memory things in the back seat. The Escalade has Dad's collection of paintings. I took them off the walls and packed them very carefully. His books and golf clubs are surrounding the treadmill, which I moved out here all by myself. The Mercedes has all of my favorite things, like our baby books and photo albums and Christmas decorations. I got my mom and dad's Bibles, plus all of their important documents."

"Do you need to gather anything else?" asked Jesse.

"Well just the clothes I was going to wear tomorrow, and my backpack and bathroom supplies," said Debra. "I'll hurry and get them." Debra came back quickly with the things and three sets of keys. "I'll drive the Escalade since I've driven it before. I do have my temps, you know." She handed the other two sets of keys to Jesse and Heather.

"What about my car?" asked Heather.

"Let's move Debra's cars first," said Jesse. "Don't worry. I live very close to here. You and I can come back here for your car. Is that OK?"

Heather understood, so they drove Debra's three cars home, and put them in Jesse's three-car garage. They noticed that his yard was full of cars. Jesse certainly wasn't alone anymore.

Brook ran up and met the girls. "I have room for a car in my garage if you need it," Brook said.

"Oh, that would be wonderful," said Debra. "The car I left at the church is full of my brother and sister's special things. I guess they aren't coming back, but I just couldn't leave their things in the house to get swallowed up by the sludge." Tears ran down Debra's cheeks at the thought of her siblings.

"Well, there's something I didn't tell you, Jesse, because I didn't know," said Brook. "My sister and brother-in-law are nurses in Columbus. I just kept thinking they were working at the hospital and didn't have time to answer my calls. But they never did call. Except for a few relatives, I'm alone in the world."

"Both Debra and Heather are all alone too," said Jesse.

"Would you two like to move in with me?" asked Brook. "If the sludge gets this far, I can go to my grandparents' farm and you can go with me. They know I might come." The two girls liked the idea.

"Heather and I are going back to get her car," said Jesse. "We should be back in about twenty minutes. Brook, why don't you take Debra and her sleep things to your house and show her around, and then meet us at my house for snacks and share time?"

Jesse and Heather went to get her car and were met by guards who didn't want to let them by, because the sludge had entered the neighborhood. Jesse told them the address, and said they were just going to get a car they left there. They were let in and were soon heading back to Jesse's house.

The house was full of people. Will, Andrew, Danny, and Larry purchased muffins and made a big pot of coffee. Matt and Lori moved Nick's mom and his younger brother into Amy's old bedroom and made up the two sofas for Nick and his other brother to sleep on. They laid out towels and washcloths and showed them around the house.

Debra and Heather had a snack and were all ready to go with Brook to her house, when Jesse stopped them. "Let's all go in the living room and reflect on our day," he said.

Some sat on sofas and some sat on the floor. They decided that everyone would share one thing, either a concern, a blessing, or just something that happened that day. Matt went first.

He could talk freely since Rosemary had gone straight to bed when they got back from the church. "My wife, Rosemary, is scared out of her mind about the sludge, and she's angry with me that we didn't leave already to go home or anywhere but here. I don't know how to get her interested in the job at hand, which is reaching others for Christ."

Lori was sitting next to her dad and she went next. "Mom will never understand the job at hand until she accepts Christ. I do have another concern though. When we went back to Rachel's house, where Ken and I were staying, and there was a note on the door. It said to prepare to move out soon, because the sludge was heading that way. Well Ken and I went ahead and moved back here, but we haven't heard anything from Josh and Rachel."

"I'm sure they're fine," Ken said. "They are probably filling her car with all kinds of things and then they will probably come here. But I have something else to share. I called my sister today. Lori and I borrowed her car and it's gone, blown away with the tornado. So we finally decided to tell her that. But she said they have worse problems than that. There is some kind of flu going around down there, and people are dying from it. They are afraid to leave the house."

"We will be sure to add that to our prayer list," said Jesse. "I need Victoria here to record everything. I guess you and your mom are next, Nick."

Nick's mom said, "I can't begin to tell you how thankful we are to you guys. You moved us out and took us in. Bless you!"

Nick said, "Yes, thank you so much. My brothers are upstairs sleeping away. Anything you want me to do, just let me know."

Brook was next to Nick so she began. "Well it seems that I am all alone in the world, and so are my two new roommates, Debra and Heather."

The two girls were going to say something, but Brook remembered something. "Say, Lori, did you tell Jesse about the break-in and look for that drug they left behind?"

"Oh no. I forgot all about it," said Lori.

Matt could see the puzzled look on Jesse's face and so he said, "I forgot too. I'll check it out Jesse and fill you in later." Matt took off to search the house.

Josh, Rachel, and Seth all walked in next and sat down on the floor.

Andrew looked at them and said, "You guys are next. We are taking turns telling a blessing, a concern, or an interesting thing that happened today."

"Josh has been helping me pack my favorite things in the cars in case we have to evacuate," said Rachel. "We drove both cars over here, hoping I can just go ahead and sleep here tonight. Lori, did you and Ken get all your stuff out of my house?" Lori told her that they brought everything with them. Jesse was thinking to himself that it was going to be difficult finding a place for everyone to sleep.

Rachel continued, "Seth came along with us. Remember he's my neighbor that I met on the plane. His aunt and uncle thought it would be better to get him out of danger right away. Is it ok, Jesse, if he sleeps here too?"

"I can sleep anywhere, even on the floor," said Seth. "I can go back home and live with my mom and dad soon."

"You wouldn't believe what it's like in our neighborhood now," said Rachel. "People are really in a panic. Anyway, I didn't invite Seth's aunt and uncle, to come here. They even have his Uncle Gordon's parents with them now. Your place seems to be filling up fast."

Jesse didn't know what to say, so he just kept quiet.

Josh was next and he just said that he was thankful that Rachel went with him to his grandparent's house today and that they got back safe and sound.

Jesse, Will, Andrew, and Danny all said that they were thankful that their church was growing so quickly. Andrew knew he needed to start a morning-prayer time at his school too.

"The students in my school aren't in the evacuation area, but there are mean guys in our school too, and I'm sure many of the students lost family as well," Andrew said.

"Well don't expect your principal to be happy about

it," said Jesse, "but if you can start a prayer group, it will bring many students to Christ." The group prayed together and Andrew, Will, and Danny left, and so did Brook and the girls.

"Jesse, is anyone sleeping in the room with the red carpet?" asked Lori. "Ken and I slept there when we were here before our trip."

"No, you can sleep there," said Jesse. "I think we gave Jamie's room to Larry. Where is Larry, by the way?"

Josh ran up to Larry's room and called down, "You guys need to come up here!"

A bunch of them ran up the stairs and found Larry on the floor in his room. He was alive, but unconscious. It took a while, but they finally got him awake. He had no idea how he got on the floor.

Matt picked up a bottle of green tea on the desk. "Were you drinking this?" Matt asked. Larry nodded yes. "This is probably the drink that was left by the guys dressed in black. I looked all over the place, but I missed this." Matt smelled it. "It smells like alcohol. It must have some kind of drug in there that put you to sleep. Thank goodness you didn't drink very much."

"How did they get in here?" asked Jesse.

"All I could tell was that the back door was unlocked," said Matt. "Probably someone forgot to lock it. Brook saw them going through your yard. I guess they just walked in."

Jesse had a bad feeling. "I hope they didn't see the note you guys left me on the counter." They decided not to worry about it right now. They needed to find places for people to sleep.

They gave Seth a bed in the room that Josh was

sleeping in. Jesse almost cried when he looked in there where his niece and nephew slept when they came for visits, and he remembered how much fun he had with them. His brother, wife, and kids were here just a couple weeks ago.

Nick's mother offered Rachel a twin bed in with her, since her youngest son went to sleep on the floor by his brothers.

Jesse walked around the house, checking the doors and windows, making sure that the house was locked up tight. He went to his room. Moments ago, he was thinking of a time when his entire family was home for a visit. They cooked out on the grill, played volleyball until dark, and sat around talking and watching movies for hours. Jesse especially missed his brothers. Besides Beth, they were his best friends. Jesse was suddenly overwhelmed with the loss.

Why had he put off accepting Christ? He could be with his family right now. They were probably all together, having fun, and they were with Jesus. And Jesse was stuck here with a house full of strangers, and there were guys dressed in black who wanted to hurt him. The tears ran down his cheeks and Jesse hoped no one would come knocking on his door. He had to be strong now, because a lot of people were depending on him. He felt bogged down with the weight of responsibility. *Lord Jesus, come quickly,* he prayed. And then he thought, *Oh no. He already came. Is he coming back for the rest of us?* Jesse ran to his desk and opened his Bible.

Jesse turned to the book of Acts because he had been reading it with Andrew and Will. He began reading in Acts 1:9. "After he said this, he was taken up before their very eyes, and a cloud hid him from their sight. They were looking intently up into the sky as he was going, when suddenly two men dressed in white stood beside them. 'Men of Galilee' they said, 'why do you stand here looking into the sky? This same Jesus, who has been taken from you into heaven, will come back in the same way you have seen him go into heaven.'"

Jesse breathed a sigh of relief as he realized that Jesus will come again in the same way he left, and that hasn't happened yet. Jesse had to face the facts. He messed up big time by not accepting Christ when he was young. Now he had to grow up and stop crying about it. Jesse wanted to fall into bed, but he needed the bathroom and he needed to brush and floss his teeth. He hesitated to go because he didn't want to talk to anyone. He peeked down the hall and it was empty, so he dashed out quickly. Just then Seth came charging out of a room with a cell phone in his hand.

"Hold on a minute," Seth said to someone on his phone. "He's right here. Uh Jesse, my aunt and uncle and my aunt's friend and my uncle's parents are all in the car because they were evacuated. Every hotel is full. Can they come here?"

"Well I'm not going to turn anyone away," said Jesse. "Do they know that every bed and most sofas are taken?"

Seth handed Jesse the phone and told him to give his uncle directions to his house. Jesse took the phone and gave them directions and took another minute to make them feel welcome. Then he rushed to the bathroom to get ready for bed because it probably won't be available again for hours. Just as he finished, he could hear banging on the front door.

As the guests filed into the house, Jesse could see that they all looked grim, as if all hope was gone. Jesse knew these people needed hope more than just a place to stay. Matt came down the stairs and saw the older couple. "Claude and Ruth, what on earth are you doing here?" he asked.

"Our whole farm was destroyed in the tornado," said Claude. "We came here to stay with our son. You remember Gordon, don't you?"

Matt looked at Gordon and said, "Of course I remember you. This is Jesse, my sister Melinda's boy. He's been kind enough to take us in. Our place was destroyed by the tornado too."

"We tried to call your parents to check on them after the disappearances, but they didn't answer," said Ruth.

"Oh they disappeared all right, and so did our daughter Sydney," said Matt.

"I'm sorry for you. We lost both of our daughters' families, including all our grandchildren," said Claude. Gordon's wife started crying.

Seth put his arm around her and said, "Aunt Kathy cries a lot. I don't blame her. I miss my cousins too."

Jesse began, "Well, the living room sofa opens up into a sofa bed. Someone could sleep on the other sofa in there too." They decided that Gordon and his parents would sleep in there, and Jesse gave Kathy and her friend the recliners in the den. They said they would be fine.

Jesse finally fell into bed, mentally and physically exhausted. His muscles ached from carrying heavy loads to cars all day. This day seemed to go on and on forever, but tomorrow, he had to go to school, and deal with teachers who resented him and Pythons who probably wanted to kill him. "Lord please help me," he prayed.

CHAPTER TWENTY-SEVEN

Thursday, Day Ten

Matt got up in the early hours to get a drink of water, and he found Claude sitting alone in the kitchen. "Is everything ok, Claude?" he asked.

"Will anything ever be ok again?" asked Claude. "I didn't want to move up here. I lived in that town my whole life. Just because the house and barn and all our vehicles are gone doesn't mean we need to move away. I could have rented some equipment, because the crops are mostly still there. But Ruth insisted we come up here. We hitched a ride to Canton, and moved in with Gordon, and now look where we are."

"You know, I have an idea," said Matt. "What if you and Ruth move into Mom and Dad's house for a while? You probably know their house better than anyone. You could hire people to re-build your place gradually and you could look after your land."

"Why aren't you living there?" Claude asked.

"I don't know. We just felt called to come here, and we were right," said Matt. "We've all become Christians since we came up here. We got baptized. Well, all of us but

Rosemary. In spite of all that's happened, like losing our family and our home, we feel like we have purpose for the first time in our lives."

"Before the tornado hit, Ruth and I started reading the Bible together," said Claude. "We were crushed when Gordon and Kathy's children and grandchildren disappeared, so we started looking for answers in the Bible."

"I know Mom and Dad were always trying to get you guys to go to church," said Matt. "They were always thrilled when you went to a church dinner or a special program with them."

"We just never thought we needed God," said Claude. "Our farm always did so well. Other farmers struggled, but I had the gift. I never depended on God or gave him any praise. But even before our family disappeared, I felt empty, like everything was meaningless. I started listening to Christian radio, and then I began reading the Bible. I never told your folks, because I wasn't ready to go to church."

"If you want to see those grandchildren again," said Matt, "I suggest you make up your mind soon. I'm free all day today, because my new job starts tomorrow. We could go over to the church and get you and Ruth baptized, and then I can take you back home, and you and Ruth can take care of their house and their cats. How does that sound?"

Claude got tears in his eyes. "I would be forever grateful," he said. "I just want to go home. And yes, I want to accept Christ."

"Look there," said Matt. "The sun is coming up. How about some coffee and eggs."

"For the first time in over a week, I feel hungry,"

said Claude. "Thanks Matt. You really are a God-send."

Matt made up a big pot of coffee and cooked up a bunch of eggs and toast. Jesse came down, dressed and ready for school. He picked up the phone and called Brook and told her that if the girls want a ride with him to school, they should be ready in fifteen minutes. Brook told him they were almost ready.

Matt told Jesse about his plans to go to the church to baptize Claude and Ruth and then take them to stay at the grandparents' house.

"What about Tim, Uncle Matt?" asked Jesse.

"Oh my, I forgot all about him." Matt looked at Claude and explained, "Yesterday our son Josh took a teenager down to live at my folks' place for a while. He was in some kind of gang and he was scared for his life, so he's hiding out there. Is that a problem for you?"

"Not for me. Maybe I'll put him to work on the farm," said Claude. "It will be good for him."

The teens all left for school, and Claude went upstairs to wake up Ruth and Gordon and fill them in about the day. Matt woke up Josh, Lori, and Ken, and told them the plans and that he needed to take his parents' car. Ken called and asked Will and Danny to open up the church for them and to help Matt with the baptisms. They were happy to help.

Matt went to their room to grab some clothes and head for the shower. He was surprised to see Rosemary sitting there wide awake. He told her all about his plans for the day and asked if she wanted to go along.

"What do you think?" asked Rosemary. I need to get out of this sludge-infested area. Yes, I'll come along."

"You know, I'm not staying down there," said Matt.

"I'm just helping out Claude and Ruth."

"I know," said Rosemary. "I'll go along and decide later what I'm going to do."

"Well get ready quickly," said Matt. "We are leaving in about twenty minutes."

Gordon, Kathy, and Seth drove separately, so they could see the baptism. On their way to the church, Seth told them how Rachel had read the Bible to him on the plane, and how he was baptized just the other day. Gordon had never been to church in his life and Kathy hadn't gone for a long time. They realized that because Seth became a Christian, he was easy to have around.

Will and Danny arrived first and had the lights on in the Worship Center. The rest of them came in and went to the front of the room. Will led them by singing a praise song he had been practicing with his guitar. It was good. Then he read Matthew, chapter 28:18. "Then Jesus came to them and said, 'All authority in heaven and on earth has been given to me. Therefore go and make disciples of all nations, baptizing them in the name of the Father and of the Son and of the Holy Spirit, and teaching them to obey everything I have commanded you. And surely I am with you always, to the very end of the age.'"

Gordon and Kathy decided they wanted to get baptized along with Claude and Ruth. Matt looked at Rosemary and asked, "Aren't you ready to put your life in God's hands?"

"No. Not yet," Rosemary said. "I think I'll keep my life in my own hands."

After the service, Kathy and Gordon hugged Ruth and Claude, and said their good-byes. Claude said that with God's help, he will rebuild the farm and maybe then they can come and live down home with them.

They all waved as they left the parking lot. Then Matt said, "I'm sorry to tell you this, but the tank is empty, and I have no money. I start work tomorrow."

"Pull into that station up ahead," said Claude. "We'll fill your tank and later on, we can stop at my favorite restaurant for lunch. We are going to pay you rent too, you know."

"Oh no, Claude, I wanted to let you and Ruth stay in the house. Mom and Dad would have wanted it," said Matt.

"Well, you guys could use a little cash, and we can spare it, so I don't want to hear another word about it!" said Claude. "I was pretty down and out, and now I can see God's hand in all this.

Ruth, I'm going to build us a fine place, and from now on, we'll use it all to serve God." Ruth smiled back at him and took his hand.

Rosemary rolled her eyes and wondered why she had to listen to this religious talk wherever she went. She was definitely leaning toward staying in central Ohio, away from the sludge.

CHAPTER TWENTY-EIGHT

Back at the high school, things were not going well for Jesse. First thing in the morning, there were even more students in the library for prayer time. There were lots of disasters for the prayer requests, so Victoria was busy getting them ready to print. Pythons hung outside the room, angry and aggressive, certain that they were losing the battle. Even wimpy students were refusing to drink their "cocktail" and it was getting more difficult to find students alone in the building for them to torment.

At the end of the prayer meeting, the students were all afraid to leave the library, since they could see Pythons through all of the hallway windows. Victoria called down to the office for help, but the principal wasn't in the office. Suddenly they saw action in the hallway, as Pythons were pushed and knocked to the floor. The Pythons picked themselves up and left the area. The library doors opened to reveal Larry and two other security guys in tan uniforms. They were carrying baseball bats, just in case they needed them for protection.

Jesse thanked them for the help. Larry tried to give Jesse his cell phone number, so he could call quickly whenever there was trouble. But Jesse explained that he hadn't bought a phone yet. Larry was very angry about the drink the Pythons left for him at the house, so he was more determined than ever to protect the students.

Jesse went to American History class, expecting the teacher to make fun of him again, but this time, the teacher was very grouchy, and didn't pay any attention to him. Someone asked him what was wrong.

"Oh, rescue workers banged on our door in the middle of the night and forced us to evacuate our house. We had to sleep in the high school parking lot the rest of the night," said the teacher. "I took a shower in the locker room this morning, but hanging out in the car, are my wife, my mother-in-law, and two dogs. So don't ask me any stupid questions today, if you know what's good for you."

Jesse decided to take a chance and raise his hand. "Ah, Mr. Gibbons, I'm really sorry for your problems. I have taken three families into my home in the past couple days. I'm sure someone would be glad to take in your family as well."

"What? Are you serious? My own brother won't take us in. Do you really think anyone else will?" asked Mr. Gibbons.

Jesse was surprised at the harshness in his teacher's voice, so he just looked down and said softly, "I'll ask around and see what I can find."

The teacher just shook his head, laughed a little, and went on with class. Later on, he started calling Jesse "Prayer Boy" again, but this time the other students didn't laugh. They looked nervously at Jesse. Out in the hall after class, one of the students told Jesse that tomorrow he will visit his prayer meeting.

Jesse was rejoicing at the news as he went charging

around the corner to his next class, and he nearly ran into three Pythons. Jesse kept his head down and slid past them, but then they recognized him and turned to follow him. Jesse ran to his next class, and just as he turned to go in the room, one of the guys in black slammed Jesse's body into the door frame. Jesse sat down in his seat, holding his aching head and ear, and he wondered if this is how life will be from now on, alternating between triumphs and hazards.

As Jesse pondered the ups and downs of his life, a student came into the classroom and handed the teacher a note with Jesse's name on the front. The teacher called Jesse to the front of the room and handed him the note. *What now?* Jesse thought.

The note read, "Jesse. Bad news. Danny and I went to the church this morning to baptize some people, and some workers came and installed a new sign on the outside that read Delilah's Casino and Lounge. Danny called the sign company and found that they were hired by the church's bank, First National Savings and Loan. I called the bank and was told that the church missed a mortgage payment last week, so they are taking the property and planning to turn a nice profit. I was told that we have all day today to remove anything we want from the building. The two of us are on it, but we need your help after school. Will"

The news hit Jesse harder than the slam he got from the Pythons. *No church. No church. We are losing our building.* Jesse decided to sign himself out of school at the end of the period. The classes seemed pointless now, in light of the news. The first place Jesse went was to the cell phone store. He decided that they all need to communicate with each other. He bought a family plan, with a phone for himself, Uncle Matt, Lori, Ken, and Josh. Jesse never wanted Will to have to drive to his school and leave him a note again.

Jesse arrived at his home and plugged in all of the phones, so they would be charged and ready to go tomorrow. He went to his bedroom and threw himself down on his knees by his bed and prayed out loud. "How can we build your church Lord if we have no building?"

Searching through his Bible, Jesse came across the scripture in Ephesians 5:19 and 20. "Speak to one another with psalms, hymns, and spiritual songs. Sing and make music in your heart to the Lord, always giving thanks to God the Father for everything, in the name of our Lord Jesus Christ."

The scripture reminded Jesse of two thing. First, he had better get a piano from the church and bring it home, because he may need to have services in his house. The other thing was something he knew, but he often forgot. He must be thankful for everything in the Lord Jesus Christ. He must be thankful about losing their church building. Some good will come of it, and he must just wait and find out what it is.

Jesse called Andrew's house, and Will answered. He and Danny had made numerous trips to the church and back, storing most things in Andrew's garage. They had moved all of the communion trays and supplies, as well as all the offering plates. They moved a piano out of the children's department, but there were others. He also said they moved all of the sound and video equipment. Jesse agreed to meet Will and Danny at the church in a half hour.

Jesse made himself a peanut butter sandwich and a

glass of milk. Josh and Rachel walked in and Josh said, "Hi Jesse. You're home from school early."

"Yes, I came home early," said Jesse. "Our church building is becoming a Delilah's Casino and Lounge, because we missed a payment last week. They didn't even notify us."

"That's really sad Jesse," said Rachel. "But we have some good news. Josh and I went to see if my house is still there. We talked to some rescue workers and our neighborhood is safe. It has something to do with the lay of the land causing the sludge to run in a different direction. So I'll be going home, and probably Ken and Lori will move back in with me. And Seth and his family will be going home too.

"Isn't it interesting the way God works?" said Josh. "If Claude and Ruth wouldn't have come here, they wouldn't have run into Dad. They are so happy going back home and they are believers now."

"Yes. I can see God's hand in all of that," said Jesse. "And I'm trying to believe that losing our church building will be a good thing. Well, I'd better hurry. We need to get the pianos out of the building or they will just dump them. I want to bring one of them here."

"I will be glad to help you Jesse," said Josh. "I was going to go job hunting, but that can wait. Let's go."

Jesse and Josh got in the car and went to the church. On their way, they passed several police cars and ambulances heading in the opposite direction. They wondered what was going on.

CHAPTER TWENTY-NINE

Later in the day, the family met back at Jesse's place for dinner. Matt was back from his trip to his parents' house.

"Well, I drove back here all alone," said Matt.

"Where's Mom?" Lori asked.

"Well, Ruth and Claude treated us royally," said Matt. "They filled our gas tank and treated us to a delicious lunch. We went to a grocery store and they bought enough food to last a month, and took it to Mom and Dad's house. Then Ruth put a big roast in the oven and started making a pie for later. Ruth loves cooking and was happy as could be."

"But why didn't Mom come back with you?" asked Lori.

"Well, you know your mother," said Matt. "Here, she's expected to make dinner every night and serve it to us at six. There, Ruth will make breakfast, lunch, and dinner, because she loves doing it, and she will play cards in the evening with your mom. Your mom told Claude and Ruth how much she loved sitting on the beach, and they told her that maybe next January, they will go to Florida for a month and take her along."

"That sounds irresistible for Mom. I guess I'm not surprised, but Mom won't become a Christian now," said Lori.

"Claude and Ruth promised to take your mom with them to church every week and to read the Bible together every evening," said Matt.

"What about Tim?" asked Jesse. "Was he still there?"

"Yes, he was there," said Matt. "He and Claude were getting along great. In fact, Tim can't wait to start working on the farm. He didn't even ask about the Pythons. He's a lot more relaxed than the last time we saw him."

"Would you all like to see what we've been up to today?" asked Jesse.

Jesse motioned for everyone to follow him to the basement. They went downstairs and there were about thirty chairs, with a piano and a pulpit. There was a table with communion and offering trays, and there was a cross on the wall. It reminded Matt of the little church back home that he grew up in. While they were down there, Jesse explained the need to move everything out of the church building.

"We set up a church just like this in Andrew's basement and one in Earl and Wilma's house down by Dad's store," Jesse said.

"You don't seem very upset about all of this," said Matt.

"I'm adjusting," said Jesse. "I have to believe this will turn out for the best. We're supposed to be thankful for everything."

Just then they heard banging around upstairs. "Where is everyone?" Josh yelled.

"Down here," said Ken. "But we're coming up."

The family came upstairs to see a very serious Josh, holding today's newspaper. "Look here and tell me what you think about this," said Josh. He read, "A security officer was killed today at Johnson High School when a riot broke out between a bunch of students and the gang called the Pythons. Several students from both groups were taken to the hospital, many in serious condition. One teacher was injured and released. Names are being withheld until the families have been notified."

Everyone looked at each other in shock. Jesse said, "It might not be Larry. There were two other security guys who came to our rescue this morning when the Pythons were trying to hassle our prayer group."

"Well, where is he then?" asked Matt. "Wouldn't he be home by now?" Matt was beginning to pace anxiously around the room.

"He doesn't have a car," said Josh. "He's been asking different people for a lift."

"Oh, I have something for all of you," said Jesse. He gave them each a cell phone and their new phone number, which they shared with each other.

"This is really generous of you, Jesse," said Ken. "We can pay you back when we get our first paycheck."

"No, it's on me," said Jesse. "After I got pushed into a doorframe this morning, I thought we need to be able to get hold of each other quickly, and I was right!"

Lori started pulling food out of the refrigerator that she and Ken purchased earlier in the day. "Dinner will be ready in about fifteen minutes," she said.

Matt slipped away to his room. He was suddenly annoyed that Rosemary chose to stay away from them, just to get out of cooking one simple meal each day. This was not the first time he had to reassure the kids about their mother. Mostly he was worried about Larry. He prayed, "Dear Lord. You know all things. Please take care of our family. Things seem to be going out of control. Everywhere we go we are in danger. I don't know if Larry is alive or not, but I'm thankful we found our way to you. In Jesus' name. Amen."

Downstairs, Matt could hear the door slam and lot of talking. He hurried down, and there was Larry surrounded by the family. He had cuts and bruises on his face and his arm was in a sling. Everyone was firing questions at Larry and he didn't know where to begin. They decided to sit and eat their dinner.

"My friend Chris discovered a bunch of Pythons attacking students in a classroom," said Larry. "He called me and by the time I got there, Chris was already dead and a bunch of students were down. The Pythons were taking off, but they managed to smash a pipe into my arm on their way out."

"How did you get the cuts and bruises on your face?" Josh asked.

"Oh, I scuffled with a Python earlier in the day," said Larry. "It's just part of the job."

"We are so thankful you weren't injured worse Larry," said Lori. "Please be careful at the school."

"Ever since the attack today, a question has been on my mind," said Larry. "What will happen to me if I die now? Will I go where Sydney is?"

"I'm thinking, yes, you will," said Lori. She read a passage from Revelation.

"It looks like we will go to heaven when we die,"

said Jesse. "But what bothers me about that scripture is that we come out of the great tribulation. Do you think that is referring to the hurricanes and earthquakes?"

"Oh no," said Matt. "Listen to this in Matthew 24:21 and 22. 'For then there will be a great distress, unequaled from the beginning of the world until now- and never to be equaled again. If those days had not been cut short, no one would survive, but for the sake of the elect those days will be shortened.'"

"It sounds like things are going to get a lot worse," said Larry. "I could have died today, and yet things are going to get worse."

"I read a little about the tribulation today too," said Ken. "Whatever happens, we need to say 'No' about getting the number 666 on our hand or forehead, because then we would go to hell. But without the number, we can't buy food. It's going to get really bad."

"Maybe we should stalk up on food and water," said Lori "just in case we can't buy those things. I think I remember advertisements to buy barrels of food that don't need refrigerated and that don't expire. I'll check it out tomorrow."

"It's already getting bad. Listen to today's newspaper," said Josh. "The state of Ohio has issued a warning to all churches. No doctrine shall be preached that is contrary to the state-approved standards, soon to be published in all newspapers. The standards will follow the guidelines mandated at the federal level of government. And any state that does not enforce the new guidelines will lose federal funding in every area. Churches can expect inspectors in their services as soon as next Sunday, and those found guilty will be prosecuted."

"I don't understand," said Ken. "Our Constitution guarantees the right to freedom of religion."

"I heard that since many government leaders disappeared, there are major changes," said Lori, "but I never thought that meant that we will lose our freedoms."

"Oh, I get it now!" said Jesse. "Now I know why we can be thankful for Delilah's Casino and Lounge! We won't be in the church anymore. We can meet in the houses until they figure out where we are, and that could take years."

Jesse called Will, Andrew, and Danny and invited them over to discuss the things happening in the world. Josh called Rachel, and Matt called Earl and Wilma. The group met and read the scriptures, searching diligently for answers and directions concerning the great tribulation. They prayed earnestly in Jesus' name.

Matt said, "It has only been ten days since we lost our loved ones in the disappearances, and yet in those ten days we have seen worldwide catastrophes, changes in government, and evil wherever we look. If we are going to survive, we need to depend on God completely and be there for each other."

Jesse said, "Since we are going to be in constant danger from now on, let's adopt Paul's words from Philippians 1:21 as our motto, 'For to me, to live is Christ and to die is gain.'"

EPILOGUE

Many of my friends and family members believe, as I do, that Christ will snatch away the Christians in what we call "the Rapture" just before the Great Tribulation, and that it could happen at any time. In the first edition of The First Ten Days, I followed the idea that all of the children all over the world, under a certain age, disappear. In this second addition, I decided to consider the idea that the children only disappear with parents or possibly grandparents, which seems more likely to me now. But I haven't found any scripture suggesting either way of thinking.

Other friends and family members interpret the Scriptures differently, and believe that Christ will come again, but only at the time of the final judgment, and that also could happen at any time.

Either way, it is my hope and prayer that we will all be together with the Lord!